TOMORROW, UTOPIA

In Washington a high-ranking politician is murdered, whilst in Central Africa, a new virus is killing thousands of male victims. And on the internet, a group known as The Utopians grows in power. Is there a connection between all these things? Homicide Detective Ben Hicks, however, has his own problems. Meanwhile, Pentagon cryptologist Hunter McCormack witnesses the murder of a politician. Now the killers are out to silence *her* . . . and no one believes she saw the killing. Except Ben . . .

Books by Steve Hayes and
David Whitehead
in the Linford Mystery Library:

FERAL
DEAD END
FANATICS
KILLER SMILE
UNDER THE KNIFE
CAST A DEADLY SHADOW

By Steve Hayes
A WOMAN TO DIE FOR

By David Whitehead
THE FLUTTERING
SCARE TACTICS

STEVE HAYES AND
DAVID WHITEHEAD

TOMORROW, UTOPIA

Complete and Unabridged

LINFORD
Leicester

First published in Great Britain

First Linford Edition
published 2012

Names, characters and incidents in this book are fictional, and any resemblance to actual events, locales, organizations, or persons living or dead is purely coincidental.

British Library CIP Data

Hayes, Steve.
Tomorrow, Utopia. - -
(Linford mystery library)
1. Suspense fiction.
2. Large type books.
I. Title II. Series III. Whitehead, David, *1958* –
823.9′2–dc23

ISBN 978–1–4448–1077–6

Published by
F. A. Thorpe (Publishing)
Anstey, Leicestershire

Set by Words & Graphics Ltd.
Anstey, Leicestershire
Printed and bound in Great Britain by
T. J. International Ltd., Padstow, Cornwall

This book is printed on acid-free paper

Prologue

The UNHCR camp roasting beneath the broiling midday sun had originally been designed to hold a thousand refugees. Nicknamed Camp Geneva, at the last count it held more than three times that number.

In the beginning there had been an attempt to bring order to the chaos. Tents were erected in straight rows, each one designed for use by four to six people, and each with the United Nations High Commission for Refugees logo stenciled on its pitched roof. But the refugees had kept coming: not just the native Chadians who had been displaced in almost incalculable numbers by the ongoing clashes between the rebels and President Déby's government troops, but also the Sudanese, tens of thousands of whom had fled west from their own escalating conflict in Darfur.

After that, any attempt at order had been abandoned. It simply wasn't possible to maintain order when dealing with such numbers. So the once-orderly camp had mutated into a ragged sprawl of make-shift reed-and-straw shelters and tattered blankets stretched over twisted poles; and as it continued to spread untidily across the flat arid plains of north-eastern Chad, so it became the embodiment of the name by which the country had come to be known — the Dead Heart of Africa.

If Camp Geneva's inhabitants hadn't been so worn down by heat and malnutrition, there might have been a riot that noon when the white Renault Sherpa 2 bearing the black UN markings drove in from the flats to the west. Behind it followed three white Renault Kerax 6×6s bearing the same insignia.

As it was, all the refugees could manage as the convoy rolled into the compound was to watch its progress through dull eyes from which even the vaguest glimmer of idle curiosity had long-since been extinguished.

First to jump out of the Sherpa was Captain Irene Colby, She wore the 'coffee-stain' desert camouflage uniform of the United States Army coupled with the blue beret and shoulder insignia of the United Nations.

As the rest of her all-female squad jumped down from the trucks, she looked around the dusty, fly-infested camp and grimaced. Moments later she was joined by Lieutenant Maria Chavez who, reading her grim expression, said: 'Not exactly Club Med.'

Captain Colby wasn't amused. 'Cut the *Saturday Night Live* crap,' she snapped. 'We're running late as it is.' She removed her helmet, showing short tawny blonde hair, and wiped the sweat from her forehead. 'Fucking heat,' she said. 'Fucking desert.'

Lieutenant Chavez didn't say anything. She admired her superior but was accustomed to her dark moods and knew better than to prod her.

Colby glared at the hapless refugees. Her wide-spaced brown eyes were devoid of mercy or kindness. Below a hawkish thin nose was a tight, thin-lipped mouth that was equally cruel and unforgiving. 'Line them up,' she ordered. 'Let 'em know we got food, water, water purification systems, medical supplies and items for personal hygiene. Tell 'em not to worry about their ration cards — assuming they still got them — but that we'll start first with all the women with children under the age of five.'

Chavez snapped into action. Using a red and white PylePro megaphone, she spoke in Chadian-Arabic, the most popular *lingua franca* of the country, and broadcast Captain Colby's message.

As her voice carried across the camp, the gaunt, half-starved refugees slowly gathered around the trucks. Watching them, Colby was reminded of the zombies in a George Romero monster flick. For the most part the few men in evidence wore light cotton pants under cotton robes, and turbans to protect them from the pounding sun. The more numerous women were covered from head to foot in thick, colorful wraparound sarongs and scarves.

Colby watched them limp and stagger toward the trucks. If she possessed any compassion, she kept it very well hidden. All she cared about was the efficiency of the mission. She hadn't always been that way, of course; once she'd cared about human life like most other people. But several tours of duty in Iraq and Afghanistan had toughened and soured her. She'd become heartless. And she was grateful for it. She knew if she allowed sentiment to enter into her thinking she couldn't do her job. She'd seen it happen.

Standing beside her, Lieutenant Chavez was equally cold in her appraisal of the human wrecks shuffling around them. *Chad. Ay dios mio,* she hated this shithole of a country. For as long as man had recorded history it had been plagued by trouble: civil unrest and civil war, political rivalry and political corruption, slave raids, power struggles, colonial battles, repression, massacres and coup after coup. And where had it gotten them? Had anything here changed for the better?

Once glance about her gave her the answer.

Chavez was a stocky, muscular redhead whose overlarge Latin features stopped her from being attractive. As she continued to watch the unloading, her gaze settled on one of the squad-members. A young black woman had stopped handing out aid packages and was now looking at the refugees with compassion, a compassion that Chavez found disturbing.

Marching up to her, she roughly pulled Corporal Teri Pollack out of the line. 'What the fuck you doing, soldier?'

Though startled, Teri quickly recovered. 'Ma'am?'

'I'll say it plain,' Lt. Chavez said angrily. 'Bury your conscience and do your duty, soldier. We don't have time for pity, *comprende?* These poor fucks are gonna die anyway. At least this way it's for a good cause.'

Teri gritted her teeth and said firmly: 'Yes, ma'am.'

'Problems?' Captain Colby asked when Chavez rejoined her.

'Nothing I can't handle.'

Both officers suddenly noticed a haggard, gray-haired man and a younger, equally careworn nurse approaching from the long, narrow hospital tent that dominated the camp.

'What the fuck . . . ?' Colby began.

'I thought this hellhole didn't have no

doctors or nurses,' said Chavez.

'Shut up,' hissed Colby. Forcing a smile, she stepped forward to greet the man.

'Dear God, am I glad to see you,' he exclaimed hoarsely. He was sickly thin and his sunburned head was bald but for a wispy covering of dry hair. He wore a wrinkled khaki shirt and shorts held up with a belt to which he'd had to add a steady progression of inward notches.

'That goes double for me, sir,' Colby said. 'I was told these refugees had been abandoned.'

'They were, Captain. They were indeed. That's why my team and I made such an effort to get out here . . . so we could help them.'

'And you are . . . ?'

'Richard Webb. Doctors Without Borders.' He was about fifty, but years in the desert made him look older. 'This is my assistant, Nurse Daphne Redman. We were in Darfur a few days ago, tending to the civil war victims. That's when we heard about these poor devils.' He looked around, shaking his head in wonder as the soldiers continued to hand out aid packages to the refugees. 'I can't believe our luck. I had no idea the UN even knew we existed.'

'We try our best to help everyone, doctor,' Colby assured him.

'Well, your best is nothing short of a miracle, Captain. I must call the Secretary General and thank him.'

For an instant, the two officers exchanged uneasy glances. 'Before you do that, doctor,' Colby said, 'I wonder if you'd look at some refugees we passed on the way in. They're stranded in one of the limestone dunes to the northwest and frankly they're in pretty sorry shape.'

'Of course,' Dr. Webb said. 'But first I'd better tell my colleague, Dr Lyman. She's been flat on her back for a couple of days with malaria.'

He hurried back to the hospital tent.

'Go with him,' Colby told Chavez.

She nodded and hurried after the doctor.

The tent provided little relief from the merciless heat. If anything, the pitched roof trapped the dry, enervating heat, intensifying it so that the air became relentlessly suffocating. Only at night, when the desert chill struck, did the heat lessen enough for patients to breathe comfortably.

Chavez followed the doctor as far as the entrance. The flaps were up, allowing her to watch him hurry between the rows of cots to a sickly woman sleeping under an insecticide-treated net. Dr. Webb scribbled a note and left it on the table beside the cot. Then he hurried back to the truck.

Making sure no one was watching, Chavez ducked into the hospital tent and went to the sickly woman.

By now the delivery of aid was almost over. Refugees clasping bottled water and aid boxes were drifting away to paw over their life-saving bounty. In addition to all the usual items — concentrated foods, wheat flour, lentils, cooking oil, tuna, cheese, chocolate, pasta, hummus, beans and hygiene products such as detergent, sponges, wipes, garbage bags, soap and diapers — they would find a certain fortified rice-soy food product which was the main focus of Captain Colby's mission here today.

Lieutenant Chavez finally returned to the Sherpa and slid behind the wheel. As she looked at her superior, her eyes told Colby all she needed to know. Behind them, the squad climbed into the now-empty trucks. Some of the refugees stayed to watch them, waving and smiling their thanks as Chavez gunned the engine and led the convoy out into the desert.

* * *

After they dropped behind the first rise and the camp vanished from sight, Colby motioned for Chavez to stop. Behind them, the rest of the column also rolled to a dusty halt.

'Where are these refugees you wanted me to tend to?' Dr. Webb asked, peering around.

Colby turned to him, holding a Beretta M-9 semi-automatic. Coldly she shot Dr. Webb between the eyes. Nurse Redman died seconds later.

There was nothing dramatic about it.

Both victims slumped down in their seats, their eyes unfocused, blood worming from the holes in their foreheads.

Captain Colby removed the Model # 47 DefendEars plugs she and Lieutenant Chavez always wore when they knew gunfire was going to erupt in a confined space, and said tonelessly: 'Torch everything.'

Chavez jumped out and ran back to the trucks, yelling orders as she went.

Colby holstered her gun and reached for her satellite phone. When she'd finished her call, she left the Sherpa and climbed a low ridge so she could watch her squad at work. They stripped off their blue berets and uniforms, revealing unmarked desert fatigues underneath. Then with an efficiency she found pleasing, they doused the vehicles with gasoline and poured a line of fuel up to the ridge. Gathering there, they watched as Captain Colby lit her own UN beret with a lighter and tossed it onto the gas-soaked sand.

The blue flame caught immediately and chased itself down the slope toward the vehicles. It quickly spread around the tires and chassis and then, one by one, the fuel tanks exploded. The Sherpa leapt into the air and tipped forward to slam back down to earth on its roof. The heavy trucks jumped but remained upright. Soon there was nothing to see but raging flames and clouds of thick black smoke spiraling into the nude blue African sky.

Lieutenant Chavez faced her squad, who stood awaiting their next orders. She again noticed the troubled, compassionate frown on Corporal Pollack's face as she watched the flaming vehicles. Chavez went up to her and pulled her aside.

'Snap out of it, damn you! Concentrate on the goddamn mission!'

Teri looked at her, tight-lipped and mutinous. 'Yes, ma'am.'

Atop the sandy ridge Captain Colby checked her rubber-strapped Frontier wristwatch. As if on cue, an unmarked HH-33 Jolly Green Giant transport helicopter appeared in the sky to the south. Drawing steadily closer, it finally descended nearby, sand boiling up beneath its downwash.

When the chopper finally set down and its four rotors slowed, Colby led her team toward it in a crouching jog. As they climbed inside, the pilot saluted and said: 'Any collateral damage, ma'am?'

The captain shook her head. 'Negligible.'

As she took her seat in back, she and Chavez exchanged a smile that came very close to being sensual.

* * *

That evening, as the sun slowly dipped behind the camp, two refugees who also worked as orderlies entered the hospital tent to light the bio-gas lamps. When they came to Dr. Lyman's cot, they found her dead beneath her insecticide-treated netting. Neither orderly noticed that the note Dr Webb had left for her was gone. Nor did they notice that the pillow Lieutenant Chavez had used to smother her had been kicked out of sight beneath the cot.

1

Hunter McCormack glanced at her wrist-watch. She was already fifteen minutes into her regular morning run and the sun was only now beginning to rise above the Washington skyline.

Broad shoulders and slim, muscular arms relaxed, she fixed her wide-set, apple-green eyes on the wooded trail ahead and continued to jog steadily past the Navy and Marine Memorial, then on through a glade of flowering dogwood trees onto the grassy bank that ran alongside the Potomac.

Hunter was a tall, lithe woman of thirty who looked ripped in her white tank-top and blue cotton sweatpants. Since her recent attachment to the Pentagon, it had become her custom to take an early-morning run through Lady Bird Johnson Park and its surrounds. Now she could hardly imagine starting her days any other way.

President Johnson's wife had chosen the site herself in an attempt to 'beautify' the nation's capital, and on a quiet morning like this, with the wispy, white clouds painted with warm pink underbellies, the park was certainly that.

As usual, Hunter kept to a course that ran parallel with the Mount Vernon bicycle trail to her left. To her right, the pale rising sun sparkled on the slate-blue waters of the Potomac, bordered on its far side by the purplish silhouette of downtown D.C.

Traffic on the nearby George Washington Highway was light enough to be almost non-existent at this hour, and she hadn't seen another living soul since leaving her red SUV in the parking lot near the Columbia Island Marina. The morning, it seemed, was hers.

Well, almost.

As she glanced toward the river she saw a tanned, white-haired man about thirty yards out, propelling his single scull with long, rhythmic strokes. His face looked vaguely familiar, though Hunter couldn't place where she'd seen him, but if nothing else he was a fellow athlete and she waved to him. He acknowledged her with a nod and a smile . . . and for Hunter McCormack, that was how the nightmare began.

* * *

Facing front again, Senator Joe Walsh continued to row like the old Harvard graduate he was. He loved rowing. Always had. Out on the water he'd been able to find the peace and solitude a man needed in order to think, consider and plan.

He'd never understood his fascination for water. Born in landlocked Pennsylvania in 1944, his earliest interests had been in politics, history and social reform. Sport — specifically rowing — had only come along later.

During his summer breaks from the University of Pittsburgh he'd worked internships with the senators, congressmen and lobbyists he particularly admired, and after he'd received his B.A. in political science he was hired by the Catholic Church to organize and instigate a series of inner city community projects throughout the state, a job he had handled well and with reasonable success.

But Joe Walsh had sensed all along that there was more important work to be done, and that he was one of the men destined to carry it out. And since it hadn't been lost on him that a highly disproportionate number of politicians — including well over half the presidents — came from a legal background, he had entered Harvard at the age of twenty-seven and graduated three years later with a Juris Doctor *magna cum laude*.

As a junior partner in a lucrative law practice he began to immerse himself more and more in politics, first at a local level, then moving up to the state legislature. Finally his local party asked him to run for the Senate. He did, twice, without success, partly because he had never married and one thing the voters liked was a committed family man.

But Walsh was tenacious. Every time he was knocked down he got right back up, and at his third try he was finally elected to the Senate, where he took a particular interest in the reformation of ethics and health care law.

A tall, fine-featured man with a strong, well-defined jaw, Walsh still cut an athletic figure in his shorts and vintage crimson crew rowing jersey. The bronze medallion he always wore around his neck — the Harvard Medal — flashed in the rays of sunlight as he continued to row with long and even strokes.

While rowing, he glanced shoreward at Hunter as she made her way along the bank and then began to weave between the trees. She was an attractive sight, a sight he'd often seen of late during his morning row, and on impulse he decided to have a little fun with her. Digging deep, he increased his stroke count so that the scull began to pull ahead of her.

* * *

Noticing the movement from the corner of her eye, Hunter wondered if she'd read the rower's intentions correctly: was he really challenging her to a race?

His smile seemed to confirm the notion.

Immediately her competitive spirit rose to the challenge. Enjoying the distraction it presented, the feel of the wind tugging at her long, coppery gold ponytail, she relished the chance to push herself and see exactly what her body could do. She dug deeper, soon drawing level with the scull, and again waved at the white-haired man.

Smiling, Senator Walsh rowed even harder and gradually the scull drew ahead of Hunter again.

She laughed inwardly. *So you want to play, do you?*

She powered on up a slope, keeping her back straight, her arms dropping a little to swing lower and faster, her stride becoming shorter but quicker.

On the river, Senator Walsh slowed his pace until she drew level with him; then he began rowing again, driving his scull even faster.

As the boat sliced cleanly through the waves, Hunter reached the top of the slope. Not wanting to acknowledge the painful stitch in her side but knowing better than to keep up the killer pace, she grudgingly stopped to catch her breath.

Senator Walsh glanced over his shoulder, saw that she'd given up and gave a triumphant smile.

Heart hammering, lungs begging for air, Hunter straightened up and saluted him, acknowledging that he'd won . . . *this* time.

⋆ ⋆ ⋆

Still smiling, Senator Walsh used one oar to steer his scull toward a dock that extended from the wooded bank. He wanted to intercept his attractive opponent and thank her for brightening his morning.

He was almost to the dock when a hand shot up from beneath the surface, grabbed the side of the scull and tipped it over.

Shocked, Senator Walsh fell into the water. He went under, gagging on a mouthful of cold water, and quickly tried to resurface. Before he could, the scuba diver who'd capsized the scull grabbed him and pulled him even deeper.

Senator Walsh struggled to break free, but his attacker's grip was too strong. They continued to grapple, churning up the water. All the senator could see of his attacker was the black Cressi mask above the black and yellow regulator. Then he spotted the titanium XS Beta Scuba knife in the diver's hand and, alarmed, fought harder to get loose.

The knife came forward in a rush of gray-green water. Senator Walsh tried to avoid it, but the blade slashed the zipper on his SV100 Ultralight inflatable life vest. He'd forgotten that he was even wearing it. He grabbed for the lanyard, intending to inflate it while he still could.

But he was too late — the scuba diver was already tearing the vest off him, ripping it down his flailing arms and then pushing it away, beyond his reach.

Growing desperate as his oxygen reserves diminished, the Senator again lunged for the surface. It was hopeless. The diver held him firmly underwater. Panicking, Senator Walsh buried his knee in the diver's groin, doubling him over, and twisted sideways. Finally free, he grabbed the diver's air hose and jerked the mouth-piece out. At the same time, he clawed at the visor and pulled free. The diver stabbed at him, forcing the Senator to release his hold, and retrieved the mouth-piece. But by now Senator Walsh had kicked upward, toward the sun-dappled surface, hoping to survive this ungodly nightmare.

* * *

Standing atop the wooded hill, Hunter had looked up when she heard the first sudden, violent splash of water. When she saw that the scull had capsized, seemingly for no reason, she immediately thought that the white-haired man had suffered a stroke or a heart attack and began running downhill toward the empty dock. But as she got closer, he suddenly burst above the surface and she felt a rush of relief.

But in the next instant a scuba diver surfaced behind him, grabbed the white-haired man around the neck and dragged him back underwater.

Shocked, Hunter broke stride and tried to make sense of what she'd just seen. That she might be watching an attempted murder seemed so far-fetched she momentarily questioned her judgment. But then, as neither person reappeared, she stopped doubting herself and ran down toward the dock.

Before she reached it, the diver resurfaced — alone. Back turned toward her, the diver continued to hold the white-haired man under the water.

'Hey! You!' Hunter screamed. 'Let him go! Get away from him!'

The scuba diver whirled and faced her. Reflected sunlight flashed whitely across the water-streaked visor.

It was then Hunter realized that she was all alone with a killer. She halted abruptly, and for a moment stood frozen.

The scuba diver raised a hand from under the water. It held a strange-looking weapon. Bulky and black, with a cluster-barrel, it had a pepperbox snout and what seemed to be an impractically long pistol grip.

Unaware that it was a Heckler & Koch

P11 underwater firearm, Hunter still knew a weapon when she saw one and immediately started scrambling back up the slope. Slipping and sliding on the dew-moistened leaves, she seemed to lose two steps to each one she took.

The scuba diver took quick aim and fired.

There was no racketing gun-blast. The P11 didn't work that way. It was a virtually silent killer. An electrical charge generated by the battery pack housed in the grip passed through the gun and ignited one of its five cartridges. In this case the cartridge was a steel dart about four inches long — in essence a small, solid-fueled rocket with fins to help stabilize it underwater, where it was effective up to fifty feet.

Above water its range was even better — more than fifty yards. But because it was intended for use underwater, the darts tended to tumble and yaw in the air: which is why this one missed Hunter and allowed her to scramble safely over the ridge.

The other side was equally steep but

Hunter didn't dare slow down; half-running, half-stumbling, she somehow made it to the bottom without falling, never once looking back.

There were no more shots, but still she kept going, sprinting recklessly across both lanes of the George Washington Highway and ignoring the angry blare of horns coming from the early-morning traffic. Badly shaken, she ran on, across a stretch of dry grass and then into a stand of white pines.

At last she reached the lot where her SUV was parked. Unzipping her fanny-pack, she fumbled for her key. In her desperation to get the hell out of there, she dropped it. She gave a tiny gasp, told herself to calm down and picked up the key. Pressing the *Unlock* logo, she yanked open the door, jumped in behind the wheel and started the engine. Gunning the gas, she roared off.

* * *

As Hunter vanished over the ridge, the scuba diver cursed and then swam under the dock to avoid any further discovery.

Surfacing behind the bushes on the other side, she pushed her hood back revealing short tawny blonde hair that belonged to Captain Irene Colby. Taking a cell phone from her wetsuit, she speed-dialed a number. Someone answered almost immediately.

'We've got a problem,' she said, and thought with grim satisfaction: *But not for long*.

2

Sometimes Detective Lou Harper felt as if his whole life could be summed up in just six little words: *I really don't need this crap*.

He was thinking that now as he parked behind the Metro P.D. Suburban Response Unit and climbed out into the chilly Washington pre-dawn.

He looked exactly what he was — a thoroughly pissed-off man who'd just been dragged out of bed. His thinning mouse-brown hair was mussed and his pale, lived-in face was still puffy from sleep. He'd thrown an old trench-coat over his gray flannel pajamas, and unable to locate clean socks was wearing a pair of plaid Reef Chewy Sandals on his bare feet.

The two uniformed police officers leaning against the SRU took one look at him and exchanged a knowing glance. Lou immediately bristled. All right, so he didn't exactly look like Homicide's finest right now, but whose fault was that?

His partner's blue 2006 Chrysler Sebring was parked slantwise in front of the police car, its two curb-side wheels up on the sidewalk. But of Detective Ben Hicks himself, there was no sign.

Lou glanced wordlessly at the officers. One of them thumbed over his shoulder. Lou squeezed through the gap between the cars and found his partner passed out on the sidewalk. He pursed his lips and shook his head, thinking: *Aw fuck, Ben. I really don't need this crap*.

One of the police officers came over and jangled Ben's car keys in Lou's ear. It wasn't much past four-thirty: too goddamn early for loud noises like that. Lou grimaced and snatched them from him.

'Next time,' warned the officer, 'we take him in.'

'There won't be a next time,' assured Lou.

'With losers like him,' the officer said, 'there's always a next time.'

Lou wanted to tell him get lost. But the guy had done Ben a favor by turning a blind eye, so Lou gritted his teeth and kept quiet. Besides, he was right. Where Ben was concerned, there *was* always a next time.

Again he looked at his partner. Ben was an untidy-looking man in his late thirties whose clothes never seemed to fit him. Tall, lean and loose-limbed, with cropped dark-brown hair and a long, stubble-darkened face tapering to a rugged cleft chin, he was funny and likable when sober; an obnoxious pain in the ass when drunk. Presently, he lay curled on his side, where the officers had found him, an empty pint of Jack Daniels clutched in one fist, snoring contentedly.

What went wrong with you, buddy? Lou wondered for the umpteenth time. *I mean, guys go off the rails every day of the week, but you've turned it into a fucking art form*.

Ben looked as if he'd gotten dressed in the dark. His tan suit was rumpled, his red, loose-knotted knit-tie stained. His shoes were scuffed and a closer examination showed that his socks were odd, one brown and the other gray.

He hadn't always been a slob. That had just happened, the way his drinking had just happened. But that didn't excuse him or make it right.

Lou glanced around. It was lucky that downtown was almost deserted at this hour. With any luck he could get Ben and his car off the street before the commuters started showing up for work.

He took another look at Ben, then sighed, grabbed him under the arms and thought: *I really don't fucking need this*.

* * *

Some incalculable time later, Ben did the very last thing he wanted to do: He woke up.

He felt like hell and guessed he probably looked worse. Sluggishly, he glanced down at himself through bloodshot hazel eyes. He was a rumpled wreck, flung carelessly onto an old leather couch. He tried to move but it was difficult, because somewhere along the line his muscles had locked up.

Looking around, he saw the big-screen

plasma TV, sound system, the bookshelf on the beige wall and finally realized that he was in the living room of his own messy apartment. The early-morning sunshine was so bright that it bleached out the lace window curtains and made his eyes ache.

A familiar sound made him look to his left. Lou Harper sat snoring in a chair, his legs stretched out and sandaled feet crossed at the ankles. Ben swore softly. Great! So Lou had seen him in all his drunken glory — again. That meant he could expect another goddamn lecture. Worse, he knew if he heard Lou say *I really don't need this crap* one more time, he was going to punch him out.

Trying to ignore the pounding in his head, Ben wondered what the hell had happened between last night and this morning? The last thing he remembered was attending his regular Tuesday night AA meeting with his usual lack of commitment. There, in the hall, Ben had watched as a short-haired kid rose self-consciously to his feet and looking at the expectant faces surrounding him, said shyly: 'My name's Billy Padgett . . . and I'm an alcoholic.'

His admission had generated the usual polite applause, which only increased his embarrassment. Ben had clapped along with them, albeit only for appearances' sake. At the Department's orders he'd been attending these meetings now for almost a year for much the same reason.

As he lay there on the couch, listening to the city slowly coming to life, he realized just how much he'd come to hate those cozy little gatherings, with their posters encouraging *HONESTY, WILLINGNESS* and *OPEN-MINDEDNESS*, and what he considered to be the empty words of their Serenity Prayer — *God, grant me the serenity/To accept the things I cannot change;/The courage to change the things that I can;/And the wisdom to know the difference*.

Oh, the sponsors were well-meaning and sincere, the chairperson earnest and enthusiastic. And more often than not that enthusiasm rubbed off on the sorry wrecks that came looking for a cure and, occasionally, found one. But so far the cure had eluded Ben Hicks.

Apart from anything else, he didn't care about himself. He was also too damned cynical. A dozen years in Metro P.D.'s Homicide Division had done that to him. *See too much of what man's willing to do to his fellow man and sooner or later it drains you of all the faith you still have in humanity — or yourself.*

He remembered allowing the endless drone to wash over him. Who gave a hoot why Billy Whatever-His-Name-Was had turned to the bottle? No matter how many excuses surfaced, at the heart of it there was always only one true reason: because it was the only way certain people could cope with the garbage life had thrown at them. And sometimes, as he knew only too well, even the bottle wasn't always enough.

The meeting had broken up at around nine o'clock. Ben was about to leave, when he'd noticed Billy standing off to one side. Ben hesitated. He hadn't always been a loner, either. That was something else that had just happened. He'd gradually withdrawn into himself. It was better that way. It made things less complicated. Still, the kid looked so lost that Ben felt compelled to say something. Joining him, he said lamely: 'Nice going, Billy boy.'

The kid grinned, relieved. 'Thanks. I sure hope I can keep it up.'

'You'll do okay,' Ben said reassuringly. 'But any time you ever need any help, call me.' He handed Billy his card.

'Thanks, I will.' Billy looked impressed as he read the card: ' . . . Detective.'

After that Ben had gone out into the night and around the block to the row of live oaks under which he'd left his late-model Sebring. Getting in, he'd leaned back, closed his eyes and sighed heavily. Then, making sure the street was empty, he opened the glove compartment, his hand brushing against the snub-nosed .38 Smith & Wesson clamped snugly to one side, and took out a pint of Jack Daniels Old No 7. Unscrewing the cap, he toasted his reflection in the rear-view mirror. 'Cheers, you ugly old bastard.'

Then he drank.

And kept drinking.

* * *

Now, in his apartment, he slowly sat up. The room tilted unpleasantly and he had to remain still until things settled down. Finally, he got unsteadily to his feet. The room lurched around him. Again, he waited until calm returned. Then, swaying a little, he slowly headed for the bathroom, moving with elaborate care so as not to wake his sleeping partner.

A few steps from the bathroom he thought he'd made it. But then his knee bumped against a table beside the door. The lamp atop it toppled over and hit the floor with a crash. A photograph in a silver frame followed it to the carpet.

'Shit!'

In the chair, Lou jerked awake. Looking around, he saw the lamp on the floor and Ben frozen in mid-step, and angrily jumped up.

Ben had seen the look on Lou's face so many times by now that it was no longer a novelty, and he quickly raised his hands in front of him as if trying to ward off the storm that he knew was about to blow his way.

'Whoa,' he said. 'Before you go off on me, I'm sorry — '

He got no further. Lou charged at him and knocked Ben sprawling with a punch that had all of his anger behind it.

Ben hit the floor hard, no longer able to feel his jaw. He lay there a moment, having neither the strength nor the inclination to get up.

Furious, Lou stood over him. 'You know somethin', Ben? I really don't — '

'Don't say it, Lou.'

' — need this crap,' Lou finished. For a moment after he said it he appeared lost for words — then it all came rushing out. 'What the *fuck* is it with you, anyway? Haven't you screwed up your life badly enough yet? Is that why you keep going out of your way to fuck it up some more? I mean, Jesus-effing Christ! What's it going to take to satisfy you? Huh? You gonna have to drink yourself to fucking death before you're happy?' He paused, veins bulging on his temples, then added: 'Well, that's fine. That's just fucking *fine!*

Go on, you lousy fuck, just keep at it! Wallow in booze until you fucking drown! 'Cause I don't give a rat's ass anymore!'

He stepped over Ben and went to the door, raincoat flapping around his legs. 'Oh, and by the way,' he said from the doorway. 'Find yourself a new goddamn nursemaid! I just fucking *quit!*'

The door slammed behind him.

Ben winced at the sound and gingerly rubbed his tender jaw. It would have been nice to think that he was the injured party in all this; that Lou was behaving unreasonably. But he wasn't. In fact when Ben thought about it, which wasn't often, he wondered why Lou had put up with him this long.

But what could he do about it? Make another stab at drying out and this time really mean it? Not likely. The pain he felt when he was sober was too much to take. Sitting up, he looked about him. The place was a mess; as much of a mess as he was. He guessed he could fix the apartment. But fixing himself was a different story. And truthfully, he doubted if he could do it — or even wanted to.

Rising, he picked up the snapshot in the frame and looked at it.

Behind the freshly-cracked glass stood Ben and a fellow Police Academy cadet, both of them mugging for the camera. They'd just graduated and had their arms wrapped around each other's shoulders. As Ben's eyes shifted from his own image to that of Marcus Freeman, he tried to remember being that young and that naive and found it impossible.

Carrying the photograph into the kitchen, he rummaged in one of the drawers until he found a roll of Scotch tape. With it, he tried to repair the damage. When he'd done the best he could, he took the photograph back into the living room and set it on a cluttered shelf beside another framed shot of Marcus, Marcus's wife Janelle and their then four year-old daughter Jasmine.

Seeing the three of them together and so happy was almost more than Ben could stand. Even now his memories of that night were still raw wounds: the sudden boom of the blow-out, the wrench of the car dragging to the right, the prolonged scream of locked brakes, the stench of rubber frying against asphalt. And then the awful, inevitable, unstoppable moment of absolute hush before two cars collided in a wrenching, crunching tangle of metal.

Torn by the memory, Ben buckled over and sobbed into his hands.

It was never going to go away.

Never.

Oh Christ . . .

He needed another drink.

Badly.

3

As Hunter drove recklessly fast along the rural highway, she tried to make sense of all that had just happened.

It wasn't easy. She had never seen anyone killed before; not even by accident. Neither had she ever been shot at before. And both events were mind-numbing. This wasn't a movie or a dumb reality TV show. This was real life. Real *fucking* life! *Her life*! And it had almost come to a violent end. One second she'd been happily racing the white-haired man in the scull and the next, someone had drowned him and then tried to kill her!

Mention of the white-haired man made her wonder who he was — and why he'd been killed. She again tried to remember why he looked vaguely familiar. Was he a famous politician or a high-profile lobbyist; maybe even a television anchor or one of the local roving reporters? No, she was sure she would have recognized him if he'd been on one of the networks or local news programs. So, who was he then? And what had he done to be murdered?

As she searched for answers, the rural highway seemed to rush at her through the windshield. The woods on either side were just a brown-green blur. She knew she was speeding and at saner moments would have eased off on the gas, but her mind was still a scramble of thoughts and her survival instincts still urged her to get as far away as possible from the killer.

She could still barely believe this had happened. But she knew she hadn't imagined it and she knew she couldn't have mistaken it for anything but what it was: murder.

She was so caught up in her roiling thoughts that she was unaware of the helicopter that suddenly threw its shadow across the roof of her speeding SUV.

The chopper allowed her to draw ahead, and then the pilot swept the 'bird away to the left before circling back and drawing parallel again. The sniper in the passenger seat raised his telescopic rifle and took aim.

The shot, when he made it, was perfect. The front tire of Hunter's SUV's front tire blew out and the vehicle started fishtailing madly. Alarmed, Hunter fought the wheel and desperately tried to regain control of the SUV. It was impossible. The vehicle spun a final time and then veered off the road and plunged into a ravine.

Overhead, the helicopter circled slowly, rotors thump-thumping. The sniper watched as the SUV rolled over and over until it reached the bottom of the canyon and exploded. He then turned to the pilot and nodded for him to take the chopper down.

The pilot obeyed. The 'copter descended and slowly circled above the burning wreckage. Its whirling rotors whipped at the thick black smoke that billowed skyward.

There was no sign of the woman. But then, neither the pilot nor the sniper expected there to be. Strapped in by her seatbelt, there was no chance she could have survived the explosion. Even now there was probably little left of her but calcified bone and charred flesh.

The sniper pointed upward, indicating that it was time to leave. The chopper climbed high above the highway, turned east and flew off.

Save for the crackling of the flames the ravine was silent.

* * *

The U.S. Marines are fond of saying that assumption is the mother of all fuckups. The pilot and the sniper were guilty of that. They had assumed Hunter would be wearing her seatbelt. In fact, when she'd jumped in her SUV she had been too panicked to even think about buckling up. And though odds were against it, that's what saved her life. With nothing to restrain her, she'd been thrown from the SUV long before impact, and now lay bruised, bleeding and unconscious in the dense brush growing on the ravine slope.

4

When Hunter regained consciousness, she found herself on a gurney in a hectic Washington D.C. hospital emergency room. A weary, white-coated Chinese doctor with rimless glasses and garlic breath was examining her.

Relieved that she was finally conscious, he explained that a hiker had witnessed the crash and explosion and called 911 on his cell. He went on talking but his voice drifted away as Hunter, floating in and out of reality, tried to recall exactly what had happened after she was thrown clear of her SUV. She vaguely remembered landing hard on the dirt slope, rolling helplessly downhill for what seemed like an eternity and ending up in some bushes, then blacking out. When she came around, she could hear approaching sirens. Then everything went black again.

The next thing she remembered was hearing several anxious voices all around her. She opened her eyes and realized the sun was now up, its pale gold rays streaking the cloudless lavender sky. Against that sky unfamiliar faces appeared and disappeared like surrealistic images. Then pain knifed through her, followed by a sense of being lifted onto a stretcher and carried up the slope to an ambulance parked on the highway. She couldn't be certain if she told the paramedics what she'd witnessed at the park and asked them to call the police, but thought she had. It didn't matter. She could always tell someone later.

Now, as the Chinese doctor stepped back and spoke to an equally weary nurse, Hunter wondered if the paramedics had obeyed her or decided she was hallucinating and said nothing.

A voice interrupted her thoughts. It was the doctor saying how lucky she was not to have broken anything. To have survived a high-speed accident such as hers and to come out of it with nothing more than bruises and abrasions — and possibly a mild concussion — well, it was nothing short of a miracle.

Hunter was not in the mood for miracles. She was too angry and too shaken. She wanted to tell him that it wasn't an accident, that someone had tried to kill her, but suddenly she felt deadly tired. She fought to stay awake but her eyes closed and she drifted off.

When she next awoke, two world weary-looking men in creased suits pushed through the curtain around her bed and smiled at her. One of them flashed his shield and introduced himself as Detective Lou Harper, and his partner as Ben Hicks. He then asked her if she would mind answering a few questions.

'No,' she heard herself say. 'Go ahead. I wanted to talk to you anyway.'

'About what?'

'I saw a man killed — drowned by another man, a diver in a wetsuit, who then shot at me and — '

'Oh, yeah, that,' Detective Harper said, cutting in. He sighed as if she'd added to his already burgeoning troubles. 'The paramedics told us about that. Said you also mentioned something about helicopters and some other guys shooting at you.

That correct, ma'am?'

Hunter hadn't remembered saying that to the paramedics, but she nodded and said: 'Yes.'

The two cops swapped dubious glances and the one called Hicks said: 'These guys in the chopper, the ones supposedly shooting at you, you any idea who they are?'

Hunter bristled. 'No, and they weren't 'supposedly' shooting at me, detective. They *were* shooting at me.'

'Did you happen to see their faces?'

'Yes, but — well, not close enough to describe them. I mean, I was driving and trying to watch the road, and . . . and the helicopter went by so fast, I — '

'Why would they be shooting at you? Any idea?'

'That's pretty obvious, isn't it? Because I saw that white-haired man murdered by the river.'

'So you think the two incidents are related?'

'Don't you? I mean, why else would they try to kill me?'

'Why else indeed,' Detective Harper

said, as if he were listening to a child telling a fairy story. Checking his notes, he added: 'That's Ladybird Johnson Park, right?'

'Yes. I run there along the river every morning.'

'*Every* morning, ma'am?'

'Yes. Pretty much.'

'And this man you think you saw drowned — '

'*Did* see drowned,' Hunter corrected irritably.

' — he runs there with you?'

'No. He rows, out on the water.'

'So you've seen him before?'

'A few times, yes.'

'But he never runs with you?'

'I just said he didn't.'

'Uh-huh,' Detective Hicks said, fighting not to yawn. 'So you're not having an affair with him or anything?'

''Course not!'

'We'll find out later if you were, you know.'

Hunter said angrily: 'I am not sleeping with him or anyone else. My God, I don't even know the guy. And even if I did, he's old enough to be my father.'

Both detectives were silent a moment.

Hunter read the doubt on their faces. 'You don't seem to believe me.'

'Well,' Detective Harper said reasonably, 'we covered the area where you claim the murder occurred and couldn't find anything to back up your statement. No trace of bullets, no sign of any struggle, no boat, no body. Nothing.'

'That doesn't mean it didn't happen.'

'No, it doesn't,' Hicks said. 'But you'll have to admit that it's pretty hard to verify that a crime took place without any evidence.'

She frowned at them. 'Are you saying I made the whole thing up?'

'We're saying it's easy to see one thing and mistake it for something else,' said Harper.

'Am I imagining these?' she demanded, holding out her bruised arms for his inspection. 'And my wrecked SUV? Did I imagine that too?'

'No. But you could've lost control of your vehicle, rolled it into the ravine and don't want your insurance company to know you're responsible.'

'And that's what you think I'm doing?' Hunter said.

'Isn't it possible?'

Hunter studied both detectives, rage mounting. 'Fuck you,' she said quietly and deliberately.

Ben Hicks eyed her shrewdly. If not for the total lack of evidence, he might have believed her story, crazy as it sounded. He handed her his card. 'If you think of anything else — any kind of clue that might prove there's been a murder — call me.'

On their way out of the hospital, Lou said: 'Too bad. She'd be a keeper if she weren't a fucking nut case.'

'I wonder.'

'Don't tell me you believe her?'

'Not exactly,' Ben said. 'But I do ask myself why someone like her, someone who seems to have a lot on the ball, would make up such a wild story.'

Lou rolled his blue-gray eyes. 'Probably,' he said, still pissed at his partner, 'for the same reason that you're a lush.'

'Which is, Dr. Phil?'

'You're seeking sympathy and attention.'

'That sounds like Peggy talking.'

'Well, she is a psychiatrist.'

'Who thinks all cops are insane.'

'No, no, no, that's not true. She thinks *I'm* fucking insane for putting up with *your* shit.'

'She's probably right.' They had reached the glass swing-doors of the lobby. Ben paused and turned to his partner. 'So why don't you just shoot me and put me out of my fucking misery?'

'Don't tempt me, pal.'

'Hey, you'd be doing me a favor.'

Lou looked at him and expelled an angry sigh. As much as he hated Ben at times, his partner possessed a likable quality that made it hard to stay mad at him. Besides, they'd been through too much together, seen too much of life's dark and unpleasant underbelly to end it on a sour note. 'Aw, shit,' he grumbled. 'Let's go get some coffee.'

They went out into the sunshine.

5

In her Georgetown home, General Katherine Trilling was sweating her buns off on a stationary exercise bike. A former military brat, she looked more like a middle-aged supermodel than one of the top military brass at the Pentagon. But appearances were rarely more deceptive: this was one woman you fucked with at your peril.

Her cell phone buzzed. General Trilling grabbed it from the handlebars and said: 'Speak.' She listened for several moments. Finally, without emotion, she said: 'Affirmative. I'll update you as soon as the mission's complete.' Ending the call, she continued cycling to nowhere.

* * *

Later that same morning her aide-de-camp, Lieutenant Jill Avery, helped General Trilling on with her tunic and then pinned a fourth star to her epaulet. 'Congratulations, ma'am. How does it feel to be only the second woman in U.S. history to become a four-star general?'

General Trilling finished buttoning the jacket and studied her reflection in the mirror. She was pleased with what she saw. 'Do you remember the best orgasm you ever had?' she asked after a moment.

'I'll never forget it, General.'

'This is way better than that.' She paused as her cell phone buzzed again. She checked the caller ID, then said: 'Get my car ready, Lieutenant.'

After her aide had left, she answered the call. 'Speak.'

Again she listened for several moments, but this time her expression hardened. When she next spoke, her voice was threatening. 'I will not tolerate dissension, Captain. *Or* wavering loyalty. If it continues, drain the swamp.' Ending the call, she again studied her reflection in the mirror. 'It's been a long road, Katherine,' she told herself. 'But we're almost there.'

She stood at attention and saluted herself.

* * *

It was, thought Professor Anna Myorski, impossible to work under these adverse conditions. She and her staff had countless vital tests to conduct and she was being pressured to conclude the experiments and turn in the results by a confidential, predetermined deadline — a deadline she would have easily met under normal circumstances. But how could she or her staff be expected to concentrate when Biotech Industries was under siege by a bunch of ill-informed protesters who tried to storm its chain-link fences at least three times a day?

She went to the window of the top floor laboratory she shared with Dr Mai Lu and looked down at the mob crowded around the gates. They were screaming and booing and waving placards which read: NO MORE CLONING! KEEP MANKIND PURE! SHUT DOWN BIOTECH! STOP PLAYING GOD! WE DON'T NEED BIOTECH CREATING OUR FUTURE!

She shook her head. Morons! Worse than that, *uneducated* morons whose understanding and responses were governed only by emotion. They had no true grasp of what was happening here, no true grasp of its significance, its importance. Theirs was the same knee-jerk reaction she had seen so many times in the past, a reaction she'd come to despise, just as she had come to despise the illiterate bumpkins who did everything in their power to block progress at every opportunity. It was a battle science had been waging ever since Galileo tried to convince the Catholic bishops to look through his telescope. Fear, denial, adherence to tradition, a reluctance to stray too far from their comfort zone — all these things had hampered scientists for centuries. And now they were hampering her and her staff from completing an experiment that if — no, *when* — successful would change the future of humanity.

Even as she watched, some of the protesters started climbing the steel fence, still screaming their hate and disapproval of what they thought was happening in her lab. The fence finally buckled and collapsed under their weight. Everyone cheered. They then surged forward, clambering over the broken fence and on through the gap they had created.

Professor Myorski's lips tightened, but not with alarm. The fence might be stormed, but the facility itself, set in Madison, New Jersey, was virtually impregnable. As she watched, a dozen security guards ran across the parking lot, brandishing batons and riot shields. She knew they would contain the breach efficiently and violently. But what were a few cracked skulls when weighed against the future they were developing here in this room?

Vaguely bored by the sight of protesters being knocked to the ground, curling into balls and covering their heads, she turned back to the laboratory. It was large and sterile, furnished with state-of-the-art equipment that her highly-trained staff used to run their myriad tests on the variety of frogs inside the glass cases sitting atop the benches. A few stools away, Dr. Lu sat studying slides under a microscope. Professor Myorski shook her head in admiration. The brilliant Asian-American scientist, who had devoted much of her life to cloning, seemed immune to distraction.

'We're going to need a stronger fence,' Myorski thought aloud.

As usual Dr. Lu was too absorbed in her work to respond. She continued peering into the microscope lens for another moment, and then motioned her distinguished colleague over.

Myorski joined her. 'What is it, Mai?'

'Take a look.'

As Dr. Lu sat back, Myorski put her eye to the microscope and turned the wheel to bring the slide beneath the powerful lens into sharper focus. She found herself looking at a cloned frog embryo without a head. Her heartbeat quickened. Slowly she looked up and swapped a smile with her colleague. 'Today, frogs . . . ' she said softly.

'Tomorrow,' said Dr. Lu, ' . . . Utopia.'

6

When they released her late that afternoon, Hunter caught a taxi to her condominium on 39th Place in Glover Park, a quiet pleasant neighborhood with tree-lined streets just north of Georgetown. She had a year's lease on the two-bedroom, 2nd-floor condo, with hopes of then buying it, and to that end was slowly furnishing it with tasteful pieces that she knew she could live with for many years. While still at the hospital she'd notified her boss about the 'accident,' assuring him that she wasn't hurt and would be at work the next day. She didn't mention anything about the murder or being shot at and deliberately forced off the highway, deciding to wait until she was in his office where she could explain everything face-to-face.

It had been a warm day and the condo was stuffy. Hunter slid open the glass balcony door and stood there a moment, eyes closed, the fading sun warm on her face as she tried to gather herself. That's when she realized she was trembling. She took a deep breath, hoping to calm down, but instead suddenly burst into tears.

She wasn't one to cry easily. But now, unable to control her emotions, she leaned her head against the door and silently wept until she had cried herself out. She felt better then; calmer.

Deciding that a glass of wine might calm her even more, she entered the kitchen and poured herself some chilled Chardonnay. Taking it into her bedroom, she opened the window, a cool breeze fluttering her sheer curtains. Undressing, she collected her bikini, wrapped a bathrobe about her and went down to the Jacuzzi.

There, alone, she discarded her robe, turned on the jets and stepped gingerly into the hot, bubbling water. Closing her eyes, she leaned her head back and tried to unwind. It wasn't easy. Her mind churned. The water soothed her aching body but made her cuts and scratches sting. Though the pain was bearable, it reminded her of just how close she'd come to dying — twice — and she shivered. *Pull yourself together,* she chided herself. *Falling apart won't solve anything*.

Sipping her wine, she moved positions, allowing the pulsating jets to massage her sore muscles. Images of the white-haired man struggling for his life by the dock kept flashing before her, like a revolving nightmare, until she wanted to scream. Who was he, she kept wondering, and what had he done to deserve to die?

Adding to her frustration was the attitude of the police. What was wrong with those two cretins? They could see how scratched and bruised she was, how badly she'd been scared, so why the hell wouldn't they believe her story?

Her thinking suddenly stopped as she sensed she was no longer alone. She quickly looked behind her. She hadn't turned on the lights upon entering, deciding that the dimness of the room would help relax her. Now, with only the underwater lights to help her see, she saw a figure approaching, a man with one arm behind his back, the other outstretched as if to grab her.

With a tiny gasp, she backed away — but she was too late. His free hand grasped her shoulder and pulled her close.

'Hey, you,' Andy Nguyen said, kissing her on the nose. 'What's this I hear about an accident?'

Hunter sagged, relieved. 'God, Andy, what took you so long?'

'Sorry, babe. I got hung up at the Store.'

'Doing what?'

'You know, one of those last-second-must-solve-it-now-codes.' He grinned and hunkered down beside her, a tall, easy-going, likable Vietnamese who had adapted to the American culture as if it were a second skin. 'But I bought you a peace-offering.' He produced a large pizza box from behind his back. 'Forgive me?'

'I'll think about it,' Hunter said. Looking at Andy, she wondered if it was possible to care about him more than she already did. 'Does it have anchovies?'

'Anchovies, mushrooms and double cheese.'

'You might have just saved your neck.'

'Halleluiah.' Chuckling, Andy set the box down and pulled off his t-shirt, revealing a muscular torso the color of *cafe mocha*. 'Before you decide my fate, okay if I jump in?'

'Sure. But hand me my bikini first.'

'It's a little late for modesty, isn't it?'

'Great Buddha say one must pay for one's tardiness.'

'Great Buddha also say sex better than pizza.'

Hunter smiled — her first smile since the events of this morning. 'I'll be the judge of that.'

* * *

In her modest Baltimore apartment, Teri Pollack sat on the floor in the middle of the living room, her face lit whitely by the glow of the laptop screen before her. She was naked under her gold-and-purple kimono, and Alicia Keys was singing *Another Way to Die* on her CD player.

When the doorbell rang, Teri blinked stupidly. She wasn't expecting visitors and besides, she was stoned out of her skull. Stumbling to her feet, she padded to the door, where she put one eye to the peephole.

Shit.

Her first thought was that she was hallucinating. She had to be, didn't she? Why else would she be seeing Captain Colby and Lieutenant Chavez waiting in the hallway outside — dressed in olive-drab jumpsuits?

The doorbell rang again and Teri flinched. But she'd been trained well. She could not ignore the summons. Trying to pull herself together, she opened the door and tried to look casually surprised.

'Good evening, Corporal,' Colby said.

'Ma'am. What . . . uh . . . what're you doing here?'

'Lieutenant Chavez and I thought we'd check to see if you were okay.'

'Oh,' Teri said vaguely.

When no invitation was forthcoming, Colby said: 'May we come in, Corporal?'

'Uh . . . yes, of c-course . . . ' Teri stepped back and her two visitors entered. Closing the door, she joined them in the living room. Even if a joint hadn't been smoldering in an ashtray on the coffee table, the officers would have recognized the sickly sweet odor of pot.

Lieutenant Chavez said: 'Enjoying some private R&R, are we?'

Teri shrugged. 'I've been a bit stressed out lately, ma'am.'

'No problem. We all have our own ways of kicking back.'

Colby wandered around the room, as if studying the decor, until she came to a halt directly behind Teri.

'That why you missed the meeting tonight?' asked Chavez.

Teri had been expecting this. 'Yes, ma'am. I mean, no ma'am. I was . . . sick. I had sushi for lunch and I think I got food poisoning.'

'Too bad,' said Chavez.

There was a short, sharp *phut* behind Teri. Her drowsy brown eyes went wide, then fearful, then blank. She collapsed into Chavez' arms. The Lieutenant lowered her to the floor. A dark red stain was already spreading across the back of Teri's kimono.

Unscrewing the silencer on her automatic, Captain Colby moved to the laptop and peered at the screen. 'I think we got here just in time. Take a look at this.'

Chavez stepped over the corpse and joined her. What she saw made her whistle softly. Colby collected the laptop and went to the door. 'Make it look like a robbery,' she said, and left.

Lieutenant Chavez set to work.

She was thorough. Working with quiet efficiency, she tore out drawers and scattered their contents across the floor. She ransacked cupboards and closets. She emptied Teri's purse of cash and credit cards, then scattered everything haphazardly around the body, where it couldn't be missed. When she was satisfied, she left as quietly and unobtrusively as she and Captain Colby had arrived.

After she was gone, Teri Pollack moved.

It was barely more than a twitch, a sudden, temporary return to life that surprised no one more than Teri herself.

Barely conscious, she reached into the pocket of her blood-soaked kimono. With great effort she grasped her cell phone and somehow found the strength to bring it up to her face. Momentarily everything blurred. Then, when she could see again, she slowly began to text, letter by letter.

She knew she could never complete the message. But as her life finally ebbed away, she managed to hit *Send*.

Please God let the message go through.

It was her last thought this side of Eternity.

7

Munching on pizza in front of the flat-screen TV in the living room, Hunter checked her phone and frowned.

'What's up?' Andy asked.

'Teri must've texted me while we were in the Jacuzzi. I've only just noticed it. But it doesn't make any sense.'

She held the phone up so he could read the text:

TRACE HRMT22 DANGEROUS
TRUST NO ONE
UTOPIA

'What do you make of that?' she asked.

Andy shrugged. 'Spooky. But if she gets high a lot, like you said, could be she's just feeling paranoid.' Seeing Hunter's concern, he added: 'Why don't you call her? See why she didn't finish — '

The door chimes interrupted him. Rising, he went to the door and opened it to reveal Detectives Hicks and Harper.

They were the last people Hunter had expected to see. Guessing they could only be here for one reason, she got up from the couch, pulled her bathrobe a little tighter around her and confronted them. 'Did you find the body?'

'We found *a* body,' said Lou Harper, adding: 'You'd better sit down, ma'am.'

She tried to read their expressions but they remained poker-faced.

'I'll stand, thank you.'

Detective Hicks said: 'Ms. McCormack, do you know a Teri Pollack?'

'Sure. We're friends.'

'*Were* friends.'

Hunter felt something cold drop in her stomach. 'T-Teri's dead?'

''Fraid so.'

'When? . . . How?'

'Earlier tonight. Looks like a burglary gone bad. She was shot.'

After everything else that day, it was just too much. If Andy hadn't stepped close and grabbed her, Hunter would have collapsed.

'Take it easy, babe,' he said gently.

Lowering her to the couch, he sat beside her and looked up at the detectives. 'You're sure it's Teri?'

'Absolutely,' Harper said.

Hunter couldn't believe it. 'B-But I was just . . . we were just talking about her . . . '

'Oh?'

'I got a text from her.'

'We know,' said Ben. 'That's what led us here.'

'It didn't make sense. I was going to call her — '

'So you have no idea what the message was supposed to mean?'

'No.'

'Have you ever seen HRMT22 used anywhere else?'

'No.'

'Could it be a code?' asked Lou.

'Possibly.'

'I ask because that's what you do for a living, right? Decipher codes?'

'I work for the NSA,' Hunter said. 'That's all I can tell you. You want to know more, you'll have to check with my superior.'

'I'm sure we'll get around to that.'

The detectives shifted uncomfortably on their feet, watching Hunter fight her emotions.

'I'm sorry about your loss,' said Ben, 'but we've got to ask you a few more questions.'

She nodded, wearily trying to compose herself.

'How long have you and the deceased known each other?'

'Three, almost four years.'

'Then I'm guessing you knew she was into drugs.'

'I know she smoked pot, if that's what you mean.'

'And snorted nose candy,' said Lou. 'We found traces of it in the bathroom.'

'That I didn't know.'

'How about her other buddies? Were they druggies?'

'I've no idea. Teri and I met at a computer class. We had coffee and sometimes lunch, but we didn't run around together.' She eyed Ben, whom she sensed was more sympathetic than his partner, despite being obviously hung over. 'You think the burglar was someone she knew?'

'It would explain why there's no sign of a forced entry, and why she let them in.'

'Any idea who it might've been?' Det. Harper said.

Hunter shook her head.

'How about taking a guess?'

'I wouldn't know where to start.'

'What about enemies?'

'Teri didn't have any. 'Least, none that I know of. She was fun to be with and pretty much liked by everyone.'

'How about a former boyfriend who might've had a beef with her?'

'I can't think of anyone. But then, Teri and I haven't been as close lately. It might have been someone she met online,' she added as an afterthought.

'Mean some guy she hooked up with on a dating site?'

Hunter nodded.

'What makes you think that?'

'Teri was an online junkie. Joked once that she and her laptop were joined at the hip.'

Lou made a note, then asked: 'What

about regular boyfriends? Was she hanging out with anyone special, a guy she might've given a key to?'

'I don't know. But I doubt it. Playing house with Mr. Right wasn't her style. Teri preferred to play the field.'

Lou looked at Andy. 'Did you know her?'

'I met her once,' Andy said. 'Here, when she came over to see if she could fix my laptop. Remember?' he added to Hunter. 'It'd just crashed and — '

'Was she with anyone?' Det. Hicks interrupted.

'Uh-uh. By herself.'

'What's funny?' Lou said as Andy smiled.

'Nothing. I . . . just remembered something is all.'

'Share it with us. We like a good joke.'

'Wasn't a joke,' Andy said lamely. 'It was weird. Teri opened up one of her files by mistake, and there were all these freaky nicknames for boyfriends — '

Ben frowned, as if he had just jogged his memory. 'Do you remember any of them?'

'Uh-uh. I only saw 'em for a second.'

'How about you?' Ben asked Hunter.

She thought a moment before saying: 'Mr. Cuddles was one . . . Long John Silver was another . . . '

'How about 'Utopia'? Could that have been one?'

'Maybe. I don't know. But I never heard Teri calling anyone that.'

Lou said: 'Could it be the deceased's blog name?'

'If it was, she never used it with me.'

'And you've no idea why she told you to trust no one?'

'No.'

'She ever tell you that before — by email or phone or in person?'

'No. Never.'

Andy, seeing how upset Hunter was, said firmly: 'I think that's enough questions for now.'

The detectives eyed each other, nodded in silent agreement and turned back to Hunter. 'We'll be going now,' Ben said. 'Sorry we had to bring you the bad news.'

When Hunter didn't answer, Lou added: 'If you decide to leave town, let us know. We may need to talk to you again.'

Again, Hunter didn't respond.

Ben smiled reassuringly at her. 'I know your friend's message told you to trust no one, but you can trust us. That's a promise.'

He and his partner left.

* * *

A few miles away three women sat at a secluded white-clothed table between the long oaken bar and the open fireplace in an upscale Georgetown restaurant named *The Guards*. The waitress, after serving them a round of drinks, was ordered not to bother them again. The drinks remained untouched, while the two younger women spoke in low, guarded voices. The third, General Trilling, who like the others wore an olive-drab jumpsuit, studied a printout as she listened, expressionless, to what she felt were lame excuses.

Unnerved by her superior's stony silence Lieutenant Chavez licked the dryness from her lips and concluded her story: 'Up until our mission in Chad, she was a damned fine soldier. She took orders well and gave everyone the impression that she had their back.'

'Cut to the chase, Lieutenant,' Captain Colby snapped. 'Tell the general when you first noticed her resolve weakening.'

'It was in the refugee camp. I could tell she was feeling sorry for the bastards. I came down hard on her for it, and she seemed fine after that. Then on the flight home she got real quiet and kind of moody. I asked her what was wrong and she said she had a migraine. I let it go, though I thought she was lying, and then, tonight, when she didn't show up at the meeting, I suspected that her loyalty was wavering and reported her to — '

Colby cut her off. 'General, we had no choice but to kill her. Not after reading her email. And you *did* say to drain the swamp.'

General Trilling silently continued to study the printout of Teri Pollack's unfinished email. Addressed to *hunt86@worldlink.com*, the message read:

```
That HRTM22 situation I mentioned
is spiraling out of control. I'd
```

give anything to bail out, but this group is like the Mafia. Once you're in you can never get out . . .

Finally the General looked up and pinned the two officers with a cold, unforgiving stare. 'So far, you've neglected to say who the email was going to.'

'We're still working on that, General.'

'What about prior emails? Her address book?'

'Yes, ma'am. We checked everything. But Corporal Pollack hadn't emailed this person for several days, and for some reason she'd erased everything in her recycle bin.'

'Obviously she didn't want anybody to trace who she'd been emailing.' General Trilling abruptly stood up and glared at Colby. 'You enlisted this woman, correct?'

'Yes, ma'am.'

'Then for the sake of your continued good health, I advise you to find out who 'hunt86' is immediately — and terminate them.'

8

That night Hunter was too restless to sleep. Though the police hadn't said as much, she wondered if they had drawn the same conclusion she had — that the attempts made on her life that morning were linked to Teri's death.

They didn't seem to believe her story, yet they hadn't pressed her on it. She wondered why not. Did they know more than they were letting on and by giving her free rein, hoping she might provide them clues that would lead to Teri's killer? Or were they using her as bait, trying to lure whoever had tried to kill her earlier and then murdered Teri into the open?

The latter scenario seemed more logical. Though Detective Hicks had appeared nice enough, even sympathetic to her plight, Hunter was sure both men were more than capable of selling her out — which meant, she realized, she was now a moving target for unknown killers with little or no chance for a future.

Alarmed, she tried to convince herself that she was letting her imagination run away with her, but she didn't believe it and worse, it didn't make her feel any better. Every time she closed her eyes she saw images of the drowning white-haired man, the scuba diver and the sniper in the 'copter shooting at her, her SUV veering out of control and, for no reason she could think of, a bleary-eyed Detective Hicks apologizing for bringing her bad news.

Teri . . . dead.

She got out of bed. Pulling on her robe she went into the living room, booted up her laptop and logged into her email account. She clicked on *Trash* and scrolled through all her deleted emails until she came to one from Teri, entitled HRTM22. She opened it and read:

> Remember the group that recruited me last year? Well, I'm finding out it has some pretty extreme ideas I don't think I can live with. I'm no moralist — like,

I had to tell you that – but I do have a conscience. Will keep you posted. T.

Hunter sighed, then went back to *Trash* and scrolled down until she found an earlier email from her dead friend.

They call themselves the *Utopians* and they believe that a perfect society can only exist once the militants of the world are eradicated. Cool, huh?

Hunter scribbled *Utopians* on the notepad beside her and then continued reading:

The founding members are all brilliant high-profile women – lawyers, doctors, politicians, generals, scientists – full of awesome new ideas for the future. About the only thing I'm a little shaky about is the way some of the hard-core members intend to reach their goal. It's pretty extreme. That said, once I'm officially a member, I'll invite you to one of the meetings. I think you'd get a kick out of it. Talk soon, T.

And now Teri was dead, thought Hunter, and perhaps the same people who murdered Teri were out to kill her, too. It was a chilling thought; especially since there seemed little she could do to stop them.

⋆ ⋆ ⋆

Outside Hunter's condo, a shadowy figure at the wheel of a blue sedan silently watched her lighted window.

9

It was mid-morning when Erin Scudder, Chief-of-Staff at the White House, entered the Oval Office and stopped in front of the President's desk. 'You wanted to see me, sir?'

President Richard Evers laced his fingers across his hard, flat stomach and nodded. A former linebacker at Penn State, he was a tall, muscular black man with the grace and eloquence of Sidney Poitier. But no one was fooled by his subtle elegance. Friends and opponents alike knew their commander-in-chief was stubborn as hell and could drive his point home like a sledge hammer.

'Yes,' he said quietly. 'I want to know about this 'situation' in Chad.'

Scudder shrugged. 'A UN convoy was attacked and destroyed near a refugee camp four days ago.'

'Christ.'

'It gets worse,' Scudder continued. A

trim, sharp-featured brunette of forty with dark ferret eyes, she'd turned down a Rhodes scholarship to enter politics, combining brilliance and ruthlessness to rocket herself to the top. She had no friends on The Hill, and even her White House staff was wary of her hair-trigger, razor-blade temperament and unpredictable mood-swings. But they and everyone else agreed on one thing: she was perfect for the job. 'The remains of two bodies were found in the ashes.'

'Our boys?'

'We won't know their identities until the DNA comes back. But from all accounts it was an American doctor named Webb and his nurse.'

'What about UN soldiers?'

'None were found, Mr President.'

'That means one of those goddamn warlords took them prisoner and wants to bargain for something.'

'I doubt that, sir. CIA reports claim that none of the local factions have taken credit for the attack.'

'Really?'

'And here's the capper. General Dupree,

the UN Commander in Chad and the Sudan, knows nothing about any food or medical convoys in the area.'

'That's comforting! But he's looking into it, right?'

'Said he'd get right back to me the moment he knew something.'

Though there was no sense of alarm in her voice and her expression remained unchanged, the President sensed something was wrong. He eyed Scudder shrewdly for a moment before asking: 'Is this something I need to worry about?'

'No, sir. Right now, our biggest concern is the disappearance of Senator Walsh.'

'Joe still hasn't showed up?' When she didn't reply, he said: 'What're you keeping from me, Erin?'

She hesitated, wondering if she should mention it, then said: 'A young woman, a cryptologist with the NSA who's on special loan-out to the Pentagon, swears she saw someone — a scuba diver — drown Walsh.'

'Christ.'

'On the positive side,' Scudder continued quickly, 'Secret Service says D.C.

Homicide claims there was no evidence to support her story and think she cooked the whole thing up.'

'A woman with her smarts . . . why would she dream up a murder?'

'They're not sure. But she had an accident, rolled her car into a ravine near the Potomac and they think it's probably some kind of insurance scam.'

'Sounds feasible.'

Erin Scudder nodded. 'In any case, they're looking into it and promised to keep me posted.'

'Excellent.' Relieved, the President grinned. 'Maybe we should check out the local motels. Joe's probably hung over in one of them after his Wednesday night poker game.'

'Better hope so, Mr. President. We need his vote to shoot down the human embryonic stem cell bill.'

* * *

Beside the wooden dock where Hunter had claimed to see a man being murdered, Ben Hicks was combing the area for clues. Watching him from the shade of an old sycamore tree, chewing on an unlit stogie, Lou Harper, shook his head.

'I don't get it,' he said. 'What do you think you're gonna find? Even if she's telling the truth, which I doubt, we've already swept this whole area.'

Intent on his task, Ben ignored him.

'What is it with you, anyway? You got the hots for this chick?'

Ben straightened up, irritated. 'No-I-haven't-got-the-hots-for-this-chick,' he snapped. 'Which she isn't, by the way.'

'Isn't what?'

'A chick. She's way too classy for — '

Before he could finish, he slipped on the wet leaves exactly as Hunter had done the previous day and fell on his face. As he hit the ground, there was the unmistakable sound of glass breaking.

Chuckling, Lou came over and helped him up. 'You okay?'

Ben nodded and brushed the leaves and dirt from his clothes.

'Can we get out of here now, before you break your goddamn — ' Lou broke off, his grin fading as he saw something on the ground. 'Sonofabitch!' he said.

Ben looked down. The bottle of whiskey he'd been carrying in his breast pocket had broken, soaking the front of his jacket.

Furious, Lou grabbed him by the lapels and slammed him back against a tree. 'Goddamn you, you gave me your fucking word!'

'And I kept it,' Ben said. He pushed his partner away. 'I ain't had a drop since you drove me home.'

'Then why the fuck you carrying around a fifth of J.D.?'

'To prove a point.'

'Oh, this I gotta hear.'

'Up yours.'

Lou glared at him, long and hard, and shook his head. 'Fucking hopeless, man, that's what you are.' He turned and started away.

'Don't you want to hear my reason?' Ben called after him.

Lou stopped but didn't look at him.

'It's to prove I don't have to drink even when I got booze handy.'

Lou slowly turned and looked at him in disgust. 'Know something, pal? You're fucking pathetic.'

'It's true. I swear.'

'The only thing that's true,' Lou said bitterly, 'is you're one sad sorry fuck. You need help. Big time. And you won't admit it.'

Frustrated, Ben watched him go. Right then, more than anything, he craved a drink.

Reeking of whiskey only increased his craving. Walking to the dock, he took off his jacket, carefully picked the shattered glass from his pocket and threw it into a trash bin.

Finished, he was about to leave when he saw something glinting in the shallows. Curious, he glanced at it. It looked like some kind of coin. Rolling up his sleeve, he bent down and picked it out of the water.

He frowned.

It was a bronze medallion. Three inches in diameter, it had *The Harvard Medal* engraved over the university on one side, and *Veritas* inscribed over a large 'H' on the other.

Ben examined the medal, guessed that it belonged to the victim, not the wetsuit-clad killer, then dropped it into a small evidence bag and tucked it into his pocket.

* * *

In Room 2SB197, one of the Pentagon's high-security offices measuring nine feet by seven, with blank walls, soundproofing and harsh fluorescent lighting, Hunter sat at a powerful, high-tech computer that was linked to a printer and an intercom. These, the desk and chair were the room's only furnishings.

She scrolled down seemingly endless columns of ciphers, symbols and alpha-numeric designators, but nowhere could she find what she was searching for: HRTM22.

Presently, she sat back, rubbed her eyes and stretched the stiffness from her lower back. If the code meant anything at all, she was sure it had to be here. But she was also aware that everything in the Department of Defense — in fact everything in every government department in every country that had a government — was compartmentalized. And at any one time, only a handful of people ever saw the whole picture. The rest, Hunter included, saw only as much as their superiors thought they needed to see in order to do their job. And if Hunter wasn't meant to see HRTM22 — assuming it was there for the seeing — then she wouldn't see it.

But still she kept looking.

* * *

Ben Hicks sat in the outer office of Senator Walsh's office in the Hart Senate Building on Constitution Avenue, scanning a copy of the Washington Post. The headline said it all: SENATOR JOSEPH WALSH (Rep) A SURPRISING NO-SHOW AT KEY SENATE HEARING.

'Detective Hicks?'

Ben looked up, quickly folded the paper and climbed to his feet. 'That's me.' As if to prove it, he flashed his shield at the young man who'd addressed him.

'I'm Alan Fox, Senator Walsh's assistant.

How may I help you?'

'I wanted to ask the Senator a few questions, but since he's unavailable perhaps you can answer them for me.'

'I'll be happy to try.'

'While the Senator was at Harvard, did he win the Harvard Medal?'

Fox shook his head. 'Not while he was at Harvard, no. The medal came much later, after he became a Senator, in fact. You see, it's awarded for extraordinary service — fundraising, teaching, generosity, leadership, things like that.'

Ben nodded. 'You ever seen it?'

'Oh, lots of times. The Senator was extremely proud of it and always wore it around his neck.'

Ben held up the medal he'd fished from the river. 'Did it look like this?'

'Yes. Exactly. That *is* The Harvard Medal.'

Satisfied, Ben said: 'One other thing: what does *Veritas* mean?'

'Truth.'

'Thanks for your time.'

Ben hurried out before Fox could start questioning him.

* * *

Captain Colby entered General Trilling's office at the Pentagon and gave a textbook salute. But if the general was impressed by the sharp, authoritarian figure the Captain cut, it didn't show.

'What's so important you couldn't tell me on the phone?'

'Ma'am, the *hunt86* we're after is a Ms. Hunter Elyse McCormack.' She put a Xerox copy of Hunter's ID photo on the desk. 'According to her internet server she's — '

'Captain, you have your orders. Why're you wasting my time on — ?'

'General, if I may continue — McCormack is a cryptologist. With the NSA.'

That grabbed the General's attention. 'You sure?'

'Unequivocally.'

'You're right,' Trilling admitted. 'That does up the ante. Okay, what do we know about her?'

'She's something of a whiz kid. Specializes in differential cryptanalysis . . . carries Top Secret clearance . . . and presently is on special loan-out to the DOD.'

The General frowned. 'The woman's *here?*' she said in disbelief. 'In the Pentagon?'

* * *

In another part of the building, Hunter left Room 2SB197, slid her security card into the ID lock and then stepped into the elevator. She took the elevator up to the Cryptology Archives. It was a large, brightly lit office divided into cubicles. In each cubicle an employee was busily tapping away at keyboards or fixedly studying computer screens showing various codes.

As she sat before her computer, it beeped and a message showed on the screen.

ANY LUCK?

She glided her chair out of the cubicle and looked to her right. At the end of the long aisle, Andy Nguyen grinned at her.

She shook her head.

Rolling back to her computer, she typed: WE EATING IN TONIGHT?

A moment later her computer beeped

again, and a reply appeared on screen: SORRY. GOT HOT DATE WITH BELLY DANCER.

Managing a tired smile, Hunter typed in BEAST! and hit *Send*.

Yawning, she looked down at the legal pad she'd taken into the Top Secret Room with her. The term HRTM22 seemed to mock her. Irked, she grabbed her purse and coat and left without looking back.

* * *

In her office General Trilling banged the phone down and turned to Colby, still standing before her desk. 'She took off a few minutes ago.'

'Do I have your permission to leave, ma'am?'

'Go.'

Capt. Colby gave another crisp salute and turned to leave.

'Captain?'

'Yes, ma'am?'

General Trilling's eyes went flat. 'This time, dammit, no slip-ups.'

10

When Ben got back to the Metro P.D. there was a Post-It note stuck on his monitor screen. He read the message and threw it into the trash basket. Rising, he crossed the large open-plan squad room to the glass-walled office that had Captain P. Novak's name inscribed on the door.

He knocked and entered, reacting uneasily when he saw Sid Meyers occupying one of the chairs. Meyers was a skinny man in a dark business suit and tie with the personality of a weasel.

'You wanted to see me, boss?'

Captain Novak nodded. He was a hulking, sharp-featured man in his fifties, with snowy hair brushed back from a low forehead. Indicating the other man, he said: 'This is Meyers from — '

'Internal Affairs,' said Ben. 'I know. How are you, Sid?'

'Breaking even.'

'What's this about, Captain?'

'As of right now, detective, you're suspended.'

Ben frowned, though the news had hardly come as a shock. 'Why?'

'Drinking on the job,' Captain Novak said quietly.

'Repeatedly,' added Meyers.

'No doubt you have witnesses?'

'Right up the gazoo, Ben.'

Trying not to show just how distasteful he found the entire ritual, Captain Novak said: 'I need your badge and your gun.'

Ben's jaw muscles tightened. He wanted to ask who these witnesses were, as if he didn't already know, and whether or not they knew he'd been attending AA meetings and fighting his problem for so long now that it had become as natural to him as breathing. He also wanted to say that the booze never affected the way he performed his duties. But then he thought: *Aw, fuck, what's the point?* Because even as he was thinking all that, there was also a tiny voice inside him saying: *Shit, I need a drink*.

Wordlessly he dropped his badge and gun onto Novak's desk.

'Thank you, Ben.'

'This suspension, boss, how long's it for?'

'Ninety days,' Novak replied. 'After that, we'll see. It's strictly up to you.'

Again Ben fought against erupting at the injustice of it all. Instead he turned and walked out.

In the squad room, everyone seemed to know about his suspension and quickly found paperwork or conversations to spare them from having to meet his gaze.

Ben ignored them in return. Grabbing his car keys from his desk, he started out. On the way he passed Lou Harper at the water cooler and shot him a glare.

Lou bristled. 'You got something to say?'

'Now that you mention it,' Ben said, 'yeah, I have.' He looked Lou in the eye, making him squirm a little. 'And you called *me* a sad fuck?' He walked on, pushing through the swing doors and out of the squad room.

* * *

Since the unexplained deaths of Doctors Webb and Lyman, along with Nurse Redman, Camp Geneva had come under close scrutiny by the UNHCR. Unofficially, the UN blamed Chadian rebels for the deaths, though the local warlords denied any responsibility for them, and now a small detachment of UN Forces had been assigned to protect the new medical staff at the camp.

Though grateful for their presence Dr Francois Girard, another of the so-called Doctors Without Borders, was too exhausted and too inundated with dying patients to worry about his own death. Beaten down by the excessive heat, as were all of his beleaguered staff this morning, he stood there in the oven-hot tent-pole hospital and watched his two nurses tending to the seemingly endless line of sickly, emaciated patients. His faith in God was temporarily shaken. Despite the U.N., the Red Cross and the rest of the Free World's efforts and good intentions, more and more refugees were dying daily. Death was now at epidemic proportions, and there was no end in sight.

Frustrated, Dr. Girard turned back to the refugees who required his immediate attention, knowing even as he did that there wasn't much he could do for them. Whatever disease or virus they were stricken with was unknown to him or any other UN doctor, so curing them was out of the question. All he could do was to hospitalize the ones who were dying and send away the ones who were still able to fend for themselves, even if only temporarily, all the time praying that someone somewhere would be able to identify the sickness and quickly find an antidote.

'I don't get it,' he said to the nearest nurse. 'I was taught that when it walks like a duck and quacks like a duck, it *is* a duck.'

Nurse Desmarais wearily brushed a strand of damp hair back from her sweat-caked forehead. 'You were also taught that new strains of known viruses crop up all the time,' she reminded.

'*Zut*, don't go 'medical' on me, Nicole. If I'm to help these poor devils I need to think out of the box.'

He surveyed his patients with an equal

measure of sympathy and frustration. All they could do was return his scrutiny with their own blank stares, while flies crawled over them.

He wondered what they thought of him. What good is a doctor who can't cure you? Who can't even identify your symptoms?

The symptoms . . .

It has all the symptoms of HIV, he thought for the umpteenth time, *and yet it doesn't need infected needles, sexual intercourse or the exchange of bodily fluids for transmission. Seems more like a cancer, but it affects only males*.

It was true. The crude sun-baked hospital and the mass graves in the surrounding desert were filled with male patients of all ages. Females, so far, seemed immune to it.

Looking heavenward, he murmured: '*Quel type d'un blagueur malade t'est?*'

Nurse Desmarais regarded him curiously. 'What was that, doctor?'

He shrugged. 'Nothing.'

But the question still echoed in his mind.

What kind of a sick joker are you?

* * *

There was an early moon hanging over Washington, D.C. that night. Its milky light showed Ben Hicks standing before a simple granite headstone. He swayed slightly, already drunk, and silently cursed himself for coming. He had hoped to find peace of mind at the cemetery, but he now realized it was a bad call. For a moment he doubted his sanity for even considering coming here. Hell, what kind of peace had he thought he'd find by standing at the grave reading the inscription: MARCUS C. FREEMAN — 1971–2006? Had he actually thought it would make him feel any better?

Morose, he took another swig from the fifth of J.D. he'd bought on the way over. But even whiskey wasn't helping him now. In fact, it only made him angrier; more bitter.

He read the inscription again: MARCUS C FREEMAN — 1971–2006.

And then it all came roaring to the surface, so much hate and anger that he couldn't even *begin* to contain it.

'Damn you!' he yelled, throwing the bottle at the headstone.

He missed, and the bottle shattered against the next marker over, splashing whiskey everywhere.

Almost immediately a dark, furtive figure lurched out from behind the marker and sank to its knees before the spreading puddle of booze. Startled, Ben stumbled back and almost fell. He peered blearily at the figure, realizing now that it was a derelict, a wino who'd been sleeping on the grass until Ben had disturbed him.

He watched as the man — it was impossible to judge his age because he was so filthy and ravaged by years of cheap wine — started lapping up the spilled whiskey.

Suddenly Ben's anger was replaced by dismay. 'Hey!' he yelled. 'No, no, don't do that, man . . . you'll cut your mouth . . . '

He hurried around the headstone and tried to drag the pathetic creature away from the shattered bottle. But the wino fought him like some crazed animal, violently pushing him backward. Ben stumbled and fell. His head slammed on the ground and momentarily the world took a drunken tilt around him that made him feel like puking.

When the feeling passed, he got up, swayed unsteadily and fumbled out his wallet. Grabbing a handful of bills, he threw them at the wino.

The wino ignored the money and continued to lap up the whiskey.

Sickened, Ben turned away. And in that moment he realized that he had just caught a glimpse of himself in the not-so-distant future.

11

General Trilling sat in the den of her large, two-story house, staring intently at a computer screen, while on the speaker Dr Lu's voice said: 'We borrowed the technique used by the British biologist Jonathan Slack at Bath University in 1997. Only instead of destroying the cloned embryos, as Professor Slack was required to do, we nursed them along until they developed into adult frogs.'

Trilling studied the images on the screen. They were a series of blow-up slides of a cloned, headless frog embryo gradually reaching maturity.

'Is that really a headless frog?' she asked at last.

'The first one in existence, General.'

'Then I must offer you my congratulations, Dr Lu.'

Dr. Lu's image replaced the frog embryo on the screen. 'Thank you, General. Of course I could never have succeeded without the help of my esteemed colleague, Dr. Myorski.'

'Not to mention billions in 'anonymous' government funding.'

'That goes without saying, General. Without the funds and your tireless support, Biotech Industries wouldn't even exist.'

General Trilling acknowledged the compliment with a curt nod. 'What about the next stage? The engineering of headless *human* clones?'

'That is already underway. Now that scientists at the University of Texas have grown headless mice, Dr. Myorski and I can see no 'ethical reason' to wait. We're convinced that humans without brains or minds can and should be used as organ farms.'

Trilling drew a sharp breath, the excitement building in her almost sexual. 'My feelings exactly.'

Dr. Lu continued: 'Our eventual goal is to perfect the technique of cloning female eggs and cells from other female bodies, as Scottish scientists did with the ewe, Dolly. That way we'll eliminate any genetic need for male semen.'

'That day can't come fast enough for me. The more we can circumvent their interference, the more chance we have of accomplishing our mission.' She was silent a moment, then asked: 'Any foreseeable problems?'

'Just the religious outrage that's mounting in the Madison, New Jersey, area. If it spreads to other cities, I'm afraid those Bible-thumpers on Capitol Hill will kill any bill supporting human embryonic stem cell research. Then all our hard work will have been for nothing.'

'Let me worry about the Bible-thumpers, doctor. You just engineer me a headless human being and I promise you, I'll use the billions we make selling organs to rid the world of militant aggression!'

General Trilling turned off the computer and switched on the lamp beside her. Turning to her companion on the nearby couch, she said: 'Satisfied?'

'Absolutely,' Erin Scudder trembled with excitement. 'But nervous, too. If this nosy little code-chaser from the NSA ever pinpoints where the funding is coming from, you and I better start packing for Mars.'

General Trilling pressed her hand over Scudder's and left it there. 'Relax, my dear,' she said. 'She's being terminated even as we speak.'

* * *

At home, Hunter grabbed a *Lean Cuisine* dinner from the freezer and was about to nuke it in the microwave when her doorbell buzzed. Her nerves were still frazzled from the events of the previous day, and as she approached the door she grew tense and apprehensive. What if it was the people out to kill her? Warily she peered through the peep hole — then scowled.

She opened the door to reveal Ben Hicks, holding a bag that smelled deliciously of Chinese takeout.

'What're you?' she asked. 'Homicide's answer to meals on wheels?'

'This isn't an official visit,' he said.

'I figured that,' Hunter said, adding: 'My God, Detective, you look like shit.'

He shrugged in a way that could have meant anything; even an apology. If he looked like shit it was because he felt like shit. He'd spent an hour driving around, not knowing what to do with himself. Finally, as he'd always known one day he would, he ended up across the street from a liquor store, fingers clawed around the steering wheel as he fought the urge to go inside and buy a bottle.

The memory of those long thirty minutes still made him sweat. The struggle he'd waged with himself had left him shaking. It would have been so easy to cross the street, go inside and oh-so-casually ask for a pint of J.D. Then he could drink himself into oblivion and maybe tomorrow everything would look different.

But he was kidding himself. He knew from experience that nothing would look different, only worse than before.

Still, he'd really needed that drink . . .

What made it worse was there was no real reason not to indulge himself. Hell, he'd been suspended and it wasn't like he had to go to work tomorrow and pretend that he didn't have a problem. In a way,

Captain Novak and Sid Meyers had done him a favor. They were giving him the time he needed to drink himself to death and end the memories once and for all.

Finally letting go of the steering wheel, he went to open the door. But as he did, he saw himself in the rearview mirror.

Jesus . . .

The reflection he'd seen there hadn't been his own.

It had been that of the wino he'd startled at the cemetery — that pitiful wreck of humanity sucking J.D. off the surface of a gravestone.

The thought sickened Ben. His stomach twitched and opening the door he leaned out and threw up. But even vomiting didn't help. He broke out in a clammy sweat. Hands shaking, he knew that even though he'd hit rock-bottom many times before, this was the first time that he'd truly been aware of it. The realization shook him to the core. It forced him to finally admit he was indeed an alcoholic, someone who desperately needed to quit drinking or else he'd end up a derelict.

Lou was right. He *was* a sad, sorry fuck.

He thought about the man he used to be and wondered if there was any chance that he could ever be that man again. He felt suddenly terrified that the Ben Hicks he'd once been was gone for good. It was, he realized, smiling grimly at his choice of the word, a *sobering* thought.

He looked at the liquor store a final time. Then fighting down the desire to buy a bottle, he drove to the nearest Chinese restaurant, bought takeout and went to Hunter's condo. He wasn't quite sure why. Maybe it was because it offended what little was left of his pride to know that Lou and the rest of the Department considered him a detective who could no longer detect. Or maybe he felt that he'd done Hunter an injustice by not believing her story in the first place. Maybe it was both reasons. It didn't really matter. All that mattered was that he'd made that all-important first step and taken control of his life.

'Listen,' he began, 'I know I should've called first but I wasn't sure if you'd talk to me or — '

Hunter slammed the door in his face.

She was halfway to the kitchen when the doorbell buzzed again. She stopped, torn between ignoring it and answering it, then curiosity got the better of her. What was the hell was he doing here, anyway?

When she opened the door again he was standing exactly as she'd left him, clutching his takeout, and still looking like shit.

'Look,' she told him, 'I don't have to put up with your harassment. I can easily call the — '

With his free hand Ben held up the Harvard Medal.

'I believe you,' he said quietly.

'You what?'

'I believe your story.'

'Why now?'

Ben indicated the medallion. 'You been following the story on TV about the missing senator?'

'Senator Walsh? Sure. Why?'

'Senator Walsh was given this by Harvard. According to his assistant, he always wore it around his neck.'

Hunter studied Ben for a moment,

looking deep into his sad, bleary eyes. 'Are you saying it was Senator Walsh I saw being murdered?'

'It's sure starting to *look* that way.'

Feeling vindicated, she invited him inside.

Later, as she served them both from the various cartons, he told her how he'd found the medal. 'I figure the chain must've broken during the struggle and the killer didn't see the medal fall, not with all the muddy water swirling around.'

'Either that or he looked for it and couldn't find it.'

'That's possible, too,' Ben admitted.

Hunter brought a bottle of hot Saki and two tiny cups to the table, but when she went to fill his cup Ben waved her off.

'I'll stick with soda, if you don't mind.'

'You don't like Saki?'

'I love it. But right now I'm, you know, trying to lay off the sauce.'

Hunter looked embarrassed. 'God, why didn't you say that before? I would've had a Coke or something.'

She started to pick up the cups and the bottle.

'No, no, it's okay,' Ben said. 'I don't mind watching you drink.'

'Sure?'

'Absolutely.'

She sat across from him, filled her cup with Saki and they started eating.

'My folks had a drinking problem,' she said presently.

'Had?'

'Yeah. Mom got a wakeup call when dad's liver took a hike last year. Hasn't popped a cork since.'

'I love happy endings,' Ben said. He pushed his food around the plate, his stomach still in turmoil from earlier.

'Don't worry,' Hunter told him. 'You'll get your appetite back. May take a few days — it took Mom almost two weeks — but then you'll be over the hump, alcoholwise, and you'll start feeling hungry again.'

Ben managed a half-hearted chuckle. 'Guess then I'll have to worry about getting fat.'

'You keep buying this much food,' she said, indicating all the cartons, 'and you won't be able to get through the door.'

'I figured your boyfriend might want some.'

'Andy? He's not my boyfriend; he's my roommate.' Catching Ben's dubious look, she added: 'Serious. I love him dearly. But he's gay. And don't look like that. Just 'cause Andy's out of the picture doesn't automatically put you on first base.'

Ben grinned. 'You're a hard woman, Hunter McCormack.'

Hunter was about to reply when something on the TV caught her eye. She quickly grabbed the remote and turned up the volume.

Ben looked at the TV in time to see footage of two police scuba divers carrying a bedraggled corpse from the Potomac. Other law enforcement officials were everywhere.

As the sound came up they heard the female newscaster say: ' . . . body of Senator Joseph Walsh, missing since last Thursday morning, has been found. Though this is unofficial, he apparently drowned while taking his morning row. The Senator, a former Harvard single sculls champion . . . '

Hunter hit the mute button and looked at Ben. 'Next time you see your partner, tell him he owes me an apology.'

'That may not be for a while.'

'You've switched partners? Good. I never liked him anyway.'

'I've been suspended.'

Her eyes searched his lined, puffy face. 'Because of the drink?'

He didn't have to reply. The sudden hardening of his expression was answer enough.

'I'm sorry,' she said. 'I hope it's only temporary.'

'Thanks. But don't worry about it. You got more important things to worry about now — like, survival.'

'Don't think I haven't thought about that. I figure if these people are willing to murder a US Senator, killing me won't even raise a sweat.'

Ben knew she was right. 'Do you have some place else to stay for a week or two — a friend or a relative maybe? By then hopefully the Department will have come up with a lead and nailed these bastards.'

Hunter said: 'No, no one other than my

mother. And I wouldn't want to get her involved in this. If something happened to her because of me, I couldn't live with myself.'

'Understandable.' Then, as an idea hit him: 'How would you feel if I were to stay over a couple of nights; maybe escort you to and from work?'

'Thanks, that's sweet of you. But I'll be fine. No one knows who I am or where I live.'

'You don't know that. They could've gotten your address from the license plates on your SUV.'

'You mean the one I deliberately totaled in a ravine so I could collect on the insurance?'

Ben grinned sheepishly. 'Ouch.'

'Sorry. That was a cheap shot.' Her tone softening, she added: 'Look, I appreciate your concern. And if you'd asked me right after the accident or Teri's shooting I'd be making up the couch for you right now. But at the moment I think I'm okay. Anyway, I still have your card. If I get scared, I'll give you a shout.'

'Suit yourself. But as you've already

seen, these guys mean business. So if you get even the slightest hint of prowlers, or being followed, call me immediately. It *could* save your life.'

'Promise,' Hunter said. Rising, she started clearing away the dishes.

Ben rose to help her but she waved him off. He leaned on the kitchen counter and watched as she put the dishes in the dish-washer and rinsed out the empty cartons in the sink. She then asked him if he wanted to take the leftovers home. When he said no, she stacked the half-full cartons neatly in the fridge, wiped off the counter and turned out the light.

Ben sensed she wanted him to leave. 'Well,' he said, hoping she'd stop him, 'guess I'll be heading home.'

Hunter escorted him to the door, opened it and pecked him on the cheek. It had been so long since anyone had touched him or shown him affection that he stiffened almost defensively.

'Thanks for dinner,' she said.

'My pleasure. Maybe we can do it again sometime?'

'Maybe. I'm jammed at work right

now, but soon as things quiet down . . . '

'Sure,' Ben said, disappointed. 'Soon as you get some free time.

'Wait,' he added as she started to close the door. He bent down and took a short-barreled Smith & Wesson .38 from an ankle holster, 'Here, take this,' and handed it to her.

She quickly pushed his hand away. 'Are you kidding? I'd only end up shooting myself.'

Ben stood his ground. 'Either take it or I'm going to sleep outside your door. Your call.'

She saw that he meant it. 'Oh, for God's sake. All right, all right. I'll keep it. Now will you buzz off? I have to get up at the crack of dawn tomorrow and it's almost tomorrow now.'

'I'm going,' he said. But he didn't move.

Tipsy from the hot Saki, she couldn't help laughing at his hangdog expression. 'Good night,' she said firmly. Then gently pushing him into the hallway, she closed the door in his face.

12

Ben climbed into his blue Sebring and let out a long sigh. Though aching for a drink, he realized he'd been right to obey his instincts and go see Hunter instead. It had given him something else to think about other than his own problems, and more importantly it had assured her that someone believed her, even if that someone was no longer representing Metro PD.

As he fired up the engine, a metallic-silver Camry pulled up outside Hunter's condominium complex. The driver climbed out and waited on the sidewalk while his passenger came around to join him. They paused under a streetlight, giving Ben time to recognize Hunter's roommate, Andy. He and the passenger spoke briefly. Ben couldn't hear the conversation, but by their body language he sensed they were arguing. Finally, Andy turned and started up the steps to the entrance, followed by the passenger.

Ben, guessing he'd just watched a lovers' quarrel, shrugged and drove away.

* * *

Hunter was brushing her teeth when she heard the buzzer go. Thinking that it might be Ben again she padded back along the hallway and put her eye to the peephole. Andy was standing there, his hair awry.

She opened the door, wagging her toothbrush at him as she said: 'Forgot your key again, huh?'

She paused as she saw a stranger standing behind him. Knowing Andy rarely brought anyone home with him, she gave him a surprised look and then turned to the stranger. As she did Andy winced, then stiffened and collapsed into her arms. Shocked, she caught him and tried to lower him gently to the floor. But his weight dragged her down with him, and as she reached around to hold him tighter, she felt the hilt of the knife sticking out of his back.

Horrified, she jerked her hand away.

Her fingers felt damp and sticky, and as she looked at her hand she saw it was covered with blood. Unable to believe her eyes, she looked stupidly at him, as if he could explain what was going on. But all he could gasp was a single word: 'S-Sorry . . . '

The stranger now stepped around them and stood just inside the doorway. Hunter looked up, saw a young slender man in jeans and a denim jacket and at the same instant, even as she was still looking, realized that it wasn't a man at all: it was a mannish-looking blonde woman with a silencer-fitted 9mm in her right hand.

'Too bad,' Captain Colby said. 'He was a great kisser.'

She pulled the switchblade from Andy's back. Then, straightening up, she kicked the door shut behind her and locked it — all without once taking her eyes off Hunter's pale, drained face.

'Okay if I use your sink?' she asked, indicating the knife. 'I don't want to get blood on my clothes.'

Hunter, unable to find her voice, said nothing. She felt her knees buckling and knew any moment they might give out on her.

'I'll take that as a yes,' Colby said, amused by Hunter's fear. Keeping the gun on her, the captain entered the kitchen, turned on the faucet and rinsed the blade under the hot water.

'You've been a fucking pain in the ass, Hunter,' she said, adding: 'You don't mind if I call you by your first name, do you? After all the time I've spent tracking you down I feel like we're old friends.'

Numbed by Andy's death, Hunter again said nothing. But suddenly remembering Ben's gun in her purse, she started inching back toward the table, knowing she had to stall for time.

'W-Why did you have to kill him? He was just my roommate.'

One-handed, Colby wiped the blade dry on a washcloth, folded it into the handle and stuffed the knife into her jeans' pocket. ''Cause he knew what you were trying to trace,' she said.

'No, he didn't. No one does.'

'Teri Pollack did.'

Hunter's mouth tightened. 'No one *alive*.'

Captain Colby shrugged, enjoying herself. 'Ah, well, one mosquito more or less . . .'

'Mosquito?'

Colby nodded and came around the kitchen counter toward Hunter. 'My orders were to 'drain the swamp' — which means all the mosquitoes have to die.'

Hunter, now backed up against the table, tried to hold Colby's attention with her eyes as she fumbled behind her for her purse. 'And I'm one of those mosquitoes, right?'

'The most important one,' Colby said, coming closer.

'Who gave you those orders?'

'What difference does it make?'

'None, I guess. But since you're going to kill me anyway, I'd like to know who passed sentence on me.'

'Sorry. No can do.'

'Then at least tell me what the code means?'

Colby gave an ugly laugh. 'Sorry,' she repeated. 'That crap only happens on TV.'

Hunter's fingers delved into her purse, groped around, finally closed on the cold, hard steel of the .38.

'My brother's a producer,' Colby went on. 'Says whenever writers can't find a way to explain some bullshit exposition — you know, back story that they weren't clever enough to tell the viewer early on — they have the villain do it for them. 'Course, it slows down the action, but — ' She broke off, suddenly aware of Hunter's plan, and wagged the gun disapprovingly at her. 'Uh-uh. That's a no-no, honey. Now show me your hands — slowly.'

Hunter grudgingly obeyed.

'That's another thing that pisses me off about TV,' Colby said. 'The hero is always portrayed as smart and the bad guy are always stupid — '

She gasped, startled, as a hand grasped her ankle, pulling her off-balance.

It was Andy, barely alive.

Instantly, Hunter grabbed Ben's gun from her purse, aimed it at Colby and pulled the trigger.

Nothing happened.

Recovering, Colby smiled and raised her own weapon.

Desperate, Hunter swung her purse by

the strap and whacked Colby across the face. As she stumbled backward, Hunter ran for her bedroom door and slammed it behind her.

Cursing, Colby fired two slugs into Andy, killing him, and then ran to the bedroom door. She tried the handle but the door was locked. She kicked it, hard enough to break any regular lock, but the door didn't move. Guessing Hunter had wedged a chair under the handle, Colby fired two rounds through it, chest high. The bullets punched through the panels, narrowly missing Hunter, who by then was hurrying toward the open window. On the way she grabbed her laptop bag and kept running. Colby fired three more rounds into the door and then kicked the weakened area. The wood splintered and she pushed her hand through the hole and tried to pull the chair from under the handle.

Hunter, meanwhile, swung her legs over the sill and looked down into the dark alley below. She could barely make out the dumpster that she knew stood against the wall. Hoping to God the lid was raised, she took a deep breath, held it — and jumped.

The fall seemed to last forever. Then she landed atop the trash piled in the dumpster, the cushioned fall still knocking the breath from her. Knowing she had to keep moving, she slung her computer bag and her purse over her shoulder and scrambled out. She landed awkwardly on one ankle, yelped, and ran off down the alley.

Above her, Captain Colby leaned out the window and peered into the darkness. She could just make out Hunter's silhouette running along the alley. Taking snap aim, she fired twice at her.

Hunter barely heard the silenced shots. But she clearly heard the slugs ricocheting off the wall near her head. Fearing that the next shot would hit her, she sprinted desperately to the mouth of the alley.

Although Hunter expected them at any second, there were no more shots. Somehow finding the strength to run faster, she burst out of the alley into the street, and unable to slow her momentum, ran out into traffic. An oncoming car braked hard, narrowly missing her. Its driver angrily punched his horn. She kept going, dodging the traffic, until she reached the other sidewalk. There, she paused, chest heaving, and looked about her. A cab was driving toward her. She stepped into its path and flagged it down.

* * *

Midnight had come and gone. Not sleepy and craving for a drink, Ben stood in a little alcove in his apartment, soberly transferring a load of wet clothes from the washer to the drier — a task he despised. He'd tried maids. But none of them had appreciated being yelled at when he was suffering from a hangover, and had all quit. Now, as he set the timer and turned the drier on, his cell buzzed. Drying his hands on his T-shirt, he checked the caller ID, saw it was Hunter and answered immediately: 'Hi. Did I forget to leave a tip?'

He expected her to laugh. But she said only: 'Ben . . . Andy's dead.'

'*What?*'

'My roommate . . . Andy . . . he's — '

'Yeah, yeah, I know who he is. How? When?'

'Right after you left. This woman . . . she stabbed him and then . . . tried to kill me.'

'Jesus! Where are you? Where're you calling from?'

'I can't tell you.'

'Mean you still don't trust me?'

'I — I don't know what I mean. Right now I'm so fucking tired and scared and — '

'Hunter, you've got to trust me; gotta tell me where you are.'

She hesitated, uncertain. 'Sorry. I shouldn't have called you.'

'Hunter — '

The line went dead in his ear. Frustrated, he ended the call and angrily kicked the laundry hamper.

* * *

Three police cars, light-bars flashing and radios crackling, skidded to a stop outside

Hunter's condominium complex. The officers, responding to a 911 call from a neighbor who'd heard the shooting in the alley, poured out of the units, guns drawn, and cautiously surrounded the building.

On a side-street a few blocks away the same metallic-silver Camry was parked under some trees at the curb. Inside, Captain Colby finished texting on her Blackberry and sent the message:

WHATVE YOU GOT FOR ME?

A reply came almost immediately:

SUBJECT CHECKED INTO ABACUS MOTEL USING AMEX CARD. ELIMINATE.

Colby smiled. DONT YOU JUST LUV CREDIT CARDS, she texted.

13

The Joshua-Israel Synagogue was one of the few original buildings left in that part of the city — which made it a regular target for Neo-Nazis. A group of them stood before the synagogue now, waving placards proclaiming anti-Semitic views and screaming profanity. It was doubtful if any of them knew why they hated the Jews so much. They just had to hate someone, and the Jews were a handy target.

Squeezed between the temple and a modern apartment building was a small green house built in President Harding's day. Inside the house, a poker game was in progress. Politicians and lobbyists sat huddled around the living room table, cigar smoke swirling overhead.

But their mood was uncharacteristically glum. For one of the chairs remained empty out of respect for a dead comrade. A mourning ribbon was draped over it and a bottle of *Wild Turkey* and an empty glass marked Senator Joe Walsh's place at the table.

As the shouting outside grew louder and more racial, Congressman Cy Jacobs went to the window, pulled the curtain aside and looked out into the street. The Skinheads were throwing bottles at the temple.

'Nazi sonsofbitches!' he hissed. 'Why the fuck don't we round 'em all up and nuke the whole fucking bunch?'

'Let it go, Cy,' said Senator Cobb. 'Get back to the game.'

'Yeah, Cy, c'mon,' another player said. 'I gotta get home early tonight. I got a six AM tee-time tomorrow with Vic Cipriano.'

Congressman Stankowski arched one gray brow. 'More contributions to the labour union? How do you sleep at night?'

'Like a baby on Valium.'

Reluctantly, Jacobs returned to his seat.

'Aren't you staying for pizza?'

'Sure,' said the lobbyist. 'If it ever gets here.' Then, as the doorbell chimed:

'About fucking time.'

Jacobs answered the door and paid the pizza man, who handed him three flat king-size boxes, and then closed the door. The pizza man hurried back to his van.

There was just one thing wrong with the picture.

The *he* was really a *she*.

And as she got back to the van, Lieutenant Chavez peeled off her fake mustache, swapped her pizza man's jacket for a windbreaker, threw everything inside the van, locked it and then walked away.

She made it to the corner, then turned and looked back. Her lips moved soundlessly. *Five . . . four . . . three . . . two . . . one* —

The van exploded in a fireball, sending a racketing blast of sound along the street and across the city. The force of it hurled the van ten feet into the air, blazing debris showering everywhere.

The little green house was destroyed by the blast. One wall of the temple was severely compromised. And Skinheads lay dead and dying in the street.

* * *

Erin Scudder was sitting up in bed, staring at a framed, autographed photo of President Evers as she replayed a conversation through her mind again.

'You're an extremely bright woman, Erin. One day I expect you to be President. But in the interim, you'll just have to settle for being my chief-of-staff.'

'Believe me, sir, I don't call that settling.'

* * *

General Trilling lay stretched out on the couch, enjoying the relaxing after-effects of her cognac as she watched coverage of the bombing on her television.

' . . . the names of the dead are being withheld until their next-of-kin are advised. This is Kelly Carson reporting. Back to you, Janelle.'

The picture returned to the studio, where an attractive black woman in her thirties was anchoring the news desk.

'Thank you, Kelly. Great job as always,'

said Marcus Freeman's widow, Janelle. 'Now on to other, less-tragic news . . . '

* * *

The all-night diner near 18th Street N.W in downtown Washington had only two customers: an old, deaf Puerto Rican janitor munching on a cheeseburger and fries at the counter, and Ben.

Ben sat in the first booth by the door, nursing his second cup of coffee and dividing his attention between the neon-lit street beyond the window and the images on an old TV bracketed to the wall.

On-screen a rugged, sunburned CNN reporter was interviewing an exhausted French doctor at the edge of Camp Geneva. In the desert behind them, male corpses of every age were being dumped into a communal burial trench.

'Dr Girard,' the reporter said, 'everyone's anxious to know if you're any closer to discovering what's causing this baffling virus?'

Girard shook his head, his voice full of

frustration as he said: 'We don't even know what it is, let alone what's causing it. But we'd better nail it down soon, bloody soon, or every male in this camp — and God knows how many other refugee camps — will be exterminated.'

The diner door opened and Hunter entered, laptop case slung over her shoulder. Ben gestured to the waitress for another coffee as Hunter slid into the booth opposite him. She was pale and tight-lipped, and fear haunted her expression.

Ben pressed his hands over hers, smiled reassuringly. 'Don't worry. You're going to be okay.'

She nodded, though she didn't believe him. 'I'm still not sure I should've called you.'

'You did the right thing.'

The waitress brought Hunter's coffee, refilled Ben's cup and went away.

'I'm glad you finally decided to trust me,' he said. Then when Hunter didn't answer: 'And about your roommate . . . Andy . . . I'm really sorry.'

Hunter stared emptily at her coffee.

Ben pushed the cream toward her but she ignored it; ignored him. 'You know the worst part of it?' she said dejectedly. 'What I keep thinking about — over and over — I talked him into it.'

'Into what?'

Hunter showed no sign of hearing him. Then abruptly she looked up, eyes tortured with grief. 'We met at work, you know. At the water cooler of all fucking places.' She paused, and was silent so long Ben wondered if she'd decided not to continue. Then: 'I'd just been reassigned and . . . Andy had just ended a long-term relationship . . . well, actually, his lover ended it but . . . I guess we were both kind of alone, and lonely and . . . Funny, isn't it? How life throws people together, I mean.'

Ben nodded, and silently sipped his coffee.

'We clicked right away and started eating lunch and then dinner together . . . I don't know why but right off I knew I could trust him, could tell him anything, even personal stuff and he'd never give it up. Same for him with me. Weird, huh?'

Ben shrugged. 'Lucky more than weird, I'd say.'

'That's what Andy said: That we were both very lucky to have met. He was always calling us kindred spirits. Then he'd say how he'd never met anyone before that he could confide in. Not even his lovers.'

'Is that why you moved in together?'

'That was part of it. But mostly it was because I never seemed to have any money and he kept talking about wanting to save so he could open his own computer business. So I suggested we rent a two-bedroom and share expenses. He really didn't want to — he'd never had a roommate before and wasn't sure if he could adapt to having another person around all the time — you know, someone that wasn't a lover. But I assured him we wouldn't be together that much, as we both had our own lives, and if I ever got on his nerves all he had to do was go into his room and shut the door. That appealed to him, and knowing it was a golden chance to save money, he moved in with me, and . . . and now he's dead and . . . I'm alive . . . and it's my fault and I feel like shit.'

She buried her face in her hands.

'You can believe that if you want,' Ben said gently. 'But sooner or later you'll realize that you had nothing to do with his death. If Andy hadn't died that way, he would've died another. It was just his turn. And when it's your turn, there isn't anything you can do about it.'

'If you're trying to comfort me, it isn't working.'

'No words can comfort you right now,' Ben said. 'Time's the only thing that can heal emotional pain, and sometimes even time doesn't work.'

'Speaking from experience?'

'Why do you think I hit the sauce so heavy?' He absently tapped his teaspoon against his cup. 'I had a police shrink tell me once that guilt trips are easy to embrace and hell to shake loose from. But I already knew that. I'd been living with one for years.' He waited for Hunter to say something. When she didn't, and kept her gaze fixed on her untouched coffee, he said: 'Not that it's any consolation, but

Andy would be the first to tell you that it's not your fault. *Or* your doing. Just a matter of being in the wrong place at the wrong time. Serendipity.'

'Shut up,' she said, so softly he barely heard her. 'Just shut the fuck up, okay?'

He obeyed and sipped his coffee. Coffee dripped from the bottom of the cup onto the table. Ben folded his napkin in half and placed it in the saucer, watching as the paper slowly turned brown.

Hunter said: 'I never knew I could be this scared.'

Ben said: 'The first time I got into a shootout with a perp I pissed my pants.'

'You saying that just to make me feel better?'

'Uh-uh. I really did. Can hear my partner laughing to this day.'

'How about now?'

'Now I just feel like throwing up.'

There was a long silence as both were absorbed with their thoughts. 'Funny,' Ben said finally, 'I always thought I'd get used to shootouts, to killing someone who was out to kill me. But I never did. For days, sometimes weeks afterward, I'd be sick to my stomach . . . ' He paused, troubled by his memories; then said: 'I fucked up tonight.'

Hunter frowned, puzzled. 'What do you mean?'

'I was still parked outside your place when the two of them got out of the car. I recognized Andy, and because of that I didn't bother to check out who was with him.'

'You think it was the killer?'

'I'm sure of it. I thought she was a guy at the time, but . . . They argued for a few moments and then went into your building. After that I drove off.' Before she could say anything, he added: 'This woman, the killer, any idea who she is?'

'No. But she said her 'orders' were to 'drain the swamp.''

Ben frowned. 'Interesting.'

'Why?'

'That's an old adage that politicians revived after 9/11 and the Iraqi war.'

'Why would a politician want to kill Andy?'

'I'm not saying one did. I was thinking

more along the lines that maybe it had some connection with Senator Walsh's death.'

'What about the word *orders*? You think maybe she's military?'

'Could be. Was there anything else about her that might back that up?'

Hunter thought a moment. 'She was cool . . . and professional, like she'd done this before. Very hardcore. Wasn't squeamish in any way. In fact, I could tell she kind of got off on it.'

The waitress returned and refilled their coffees. Did they want anything else? No, just the check, Ben told her. She totaled their check, left it on the table and went back behind the counter.

Hunter, making sure she wasn't being watched, took Ben's gun from her purse and slid it to him.

'No, no, you keep it,' he said, 'for protection.'

'But it doesn't work.'

'What do you mean?'

'I pulled the trigger and nothing happened.'

Ben took the gun and examined it

briefly. 'That's 'cause the safety's on. Before you shoot you gotta push it down like this.'

He demonstrated twice. Then he gave her the gun, saying: 'Try it.'

Reluctantly, she obeyed. Knowing nothing about guns, she performed the maneuver awkwardly. Ben nodded for her to try again. She did, several times, until she felt comfortable doing it. Then, not checking to see if the safety was on or off, but assuming it was, she squeezed the trigger.

The gun fired, the loud booming roar magnified in the confined space of the diner, and the window beside them shattered. Shards of glass flew into the street, shattering musically into smaller pieces on the sidewalk.

Startled, Ben jumped halfway out of the booth. His knees slammed against the underside of the table, overturning their cups and spilling coffee everywhere.

Hunter screamed, without realizing, and dropped the gun on the table.

The waitress also screamed and jumped back against the coffee-maker, knocking it onto the floor.

The janitor, who'd turned off his hearing aid after ordering his meal, didn't hear the shot. But, puzzled by the waitress' behavior, he spun around on his stool to see what had frightened her.

By now Ben had stuffed the gun in his pocket, and was dragging Hunter to the door. They spilled out onto the street. Traffic was sparse at this late hour and so were pedestrians. Ben pulled Hunter to the corner, ignoring the looks from passersby, and on down the street to his parked sedan. They leaned against it, both winded, and tried to catch their breath.

'God, I'm so sorry,' she said. 'I don't know what I was thinking — '

He cut her off, 'We better get going,' and opened the passenger-side door for her.

'What about my car?'

'We'll come back for it tomorrow.'

Hunter nodded and climbed in.

Ben got in behind the wheel, started the car and was about to drive away when he suddenly began to chuckle.

She looked at him like he was crazy. 'What?' she said.

He started laughing.

'Fuck you,' she said. 'It wasn't that funny.'

He only laughed harder.

It was infectious. Hunter began to giggle, then laugh and then both of them were laughing so hard, it was all they could do not to cry.

14

Emotionally exhausted, they drove back to the Abacus Motel and flopped down on the bed to watch a replay on TV of the earlier explosion. A perky female reporter was saying: ' . . . though the police haven't made an official statement yet, the thinking here is that neo-Nazi skinheads, not terrorists, were behind the bombing.'

Hunter chewed her lower lip. 'That doesn't make sense,' she said. 'Skinheads aren't suicide bombers. They wouldn't blow themselves up just to destroy a synagogue.'

'Not deliberately maybe, but mistakes happen.'

'With dynamite?'

'You obviously never saw *Butch Cassidy and the Sundance Kid*.'

'You're comparing this to a comedy from the sixties?'

'It was based on fact. Butch and Sundance were experienced bank robbers but hadn't robbed a train before. Butch used too much dynamite and almost blew up his whole gang.' Ben shrugged. 'It's just a theory.'

'So you're saying this was a hate crime that mistakenly killed a senator and two congressmen who just happened to be playing poker in the house next door?'

'Shit happens.'

'So do coincidences. I'm just not sold that this was one. I smell a cover-up.'

'I think you mean *diversion*.'

About to reply, she noticed his hands were shaking. She didn't know how long it had been since he'd had a drink, but she realized the withdrawal was getting to him.

'You going to be okay?'

Ben gave her a tight, grim smile. 'We'll soon find out, won't we?'

'Is there anything I can do to help?'

He shook his head. She took her laptop from its case, set it on the table and booted it up.

Needing something to focus on besides booze, Ben joined her. 'What're you looking for?'

'A common denominator.'

'Between the skinheads and politicians?'

'Between the politicians. Might give us a reason why they were killed.'

'While you're at it, throw Senator Walsh into the mix — ' He broke off as they heard a car drive in. Ben signaled for Hunter to kill the light. As she plunged the room into darkness, he took the .38 from under the pillow and went to the window. Carefully, he inched the blind aside just enough to see out.

The first thing he noticed was the car: a metallic-silver Camry. Then four women got out, all dressed in olive-drab T-shirts and jeans. Each one carried a semi-automatic with an attached silencer.

Ben felt Hunter's warmth against his skin as she joined him, heard her sudden intake of breath. 'The one in the lead,' she whispered as the women entered the office. 'That's her! The one who killed Andy.'

Ben released the safety catch. 'Recognize any of the others?'

'I'm not sure. Maybe one. The redhead.'

'From where?'

'I don't know.'
'Think!'
'I *am* thinking! . . . NSA . . . Pentagon maybe.'
'So these women *are* military personnel?'
'Could be. I'm not sure. I see hundreds of people every day, in and out of uniform. For the most part they're military but we also get a lot of civilians; visitors. So she could be either.'
'Great.'
'Jesus, Ben, what do you want from me? I'm a cryptologist, not a fucking detective!'
'Okay, okay, calm down. I'm just trying to figure out the connection between you seeing a scuba diver drown a Senator and the military trying to kill you.' He broke the gun open and checked the cylinder: four rounds. It wasn't much to make a stand with. 'Not that it's gonna matter in about thirty seconds,' he concluded.
'Can't you call for back-up?'
'I'm on suspension, remember? Don't worry,' he added. 'I'll think of something.'

* * *

Captain Colby and the other women emerged from the office. Behind them, the clerk lay slumped across the desk, blood coming from a neat bullet-hole in his forehead.

The women quickly crossed the lot. Wordlessly Colby and Lieutenant Chavez watched as their two companions pressed their backs against the walls on either side of Hunter's door. Then, on a silent signal, the larger woman shouldered the door. The lock broke and the door swung inward. All four women rushed inside, guns at the ready.

The room was empty.

They flipped the light on and quickly looked under the bed. Colby and Chavez checked the bathroom. It too was empty, but just to make sure Colby fired three shots through the shower curtain and then whipped it aside.

The shower was empty. The only damage her bullets had done was to ruin the shower curtain and crack several tiles. Colby gestured at the frosted window above the shower. It was open, indicating where their target had escaped. 'C'mon,' she said. She ran from the room, Lieutenant Chavez on her heels.

As they hurried to the front door, a car started up. Jerking open the door, Colby was in time to see a blue sedan race out of the parking lot and into passing traffic.

She punched the doorframe. 'Fuck! Let's move!'

* * *

Ben weaved in and out of traffic, brakes squealing, until he had put several blocks between them and their attackers. His first impulse was to pull into a dark alley and hide until, hopefully, the killers gave up on them. But his instinct as a detective told him it was probably safer to keep on the move.

'How the hell did they know where I was?' Hunter asked as they joined several cars stopped at a traffic light.

Keeping a watchful eye in the rear-view mirror, he said: 'Get in the back seat.'

'What?'

'Don't argue. Just do it. Now. Then dump your purse out. Check everything in it. Cell phone. Wallet. Keys. Then your watch, shoes — '

'Why don't I strip while I'm at it?'

'You didn't let me finish.'

His grim look told Hunter he was serious.

Once in back, she did as he asked. When she caught him looking at her in the rear-view mirror, she said: 'Stop watching me, dammit.'

'Don't worry. You're not my type.'

'Stop flattering me.'

The light changed. Traffic in front of them moved ahead. Ben followed, keeping pace with them.

Hunter quickly searched her purse, then unbuttoned her shirt and checked her bra. Looking up suddenly, she caught him watching her in the mirror again. 'Thought I wasn't your type?'

'I guess I could be persuaded.'

'Gee, thanks.'

'Hell, if you want the truth, I'm at an age where every woman's my type.'

'Stop beating yourself up. With the right woman's touch you'd be a great catch.'

He rolled his eyes, said: 'Find anything?'

'Uh-uh. Okay if I put my clothes back on?'

He wasn't listening. 'When you called me — was it on your cell?'

'Yes, but — '

'Give it to me.'

'No, no, I won't use it again. Promise.'

'And if you forget?'

Grudgingly, Hunter handed him her cell. He pounded it against the steering wheel until it finally shattered.

'Thanks,' she said. 'Now, what?'

'Good question.'

'Well, that really builds my confidence.'

To her surprise, Ben drove them to a run-down part of town. Half the streetlights had been vandalized, making the entire area a no-go zone. Shadowy, hooded figures watched them from darkened doorways lit only by the tiny orange dots of glowing cigarettes.

At last he pulled up outside some tenements. A gang of black youths eyed them menacingly. 'Be right back,' he told her.

'Wait — '

She grasped his arm as he was opening the door.

'It's okay,' he assured her. 'I know them.'

'You know *them*, but who knows *me*?'

'You'll be fine. Trust me.' He gently unclasped her fingers. 'This'll only take a moment.' Getting out, he closed the door and walked up to the gang. The youths greeted him with surly nods. Unfazed, Ben confronted the leader and the two began discussing something.

Hunter carefully lowered the window, hoping to hear what they were saying. But they were talking too softly. Ben finally slipped the leader some cash and was given a small package in return. Nodding his thanks he walked back to the car.

'Here,' he said, handing Hunter a cell phone. 'From now on, any call you make, use that. It's untraceable.'

* * *

It was almost two in the morning when Ben drove Hunter back to his apartment. As near as he knew, no one could have linked him to her, ergo no one knew who he was or where he lived or that Hunter might be staying with him.

Once inside, Ben made some of his 'special hot chocolate' and brought the mugs to the kitchen table, where Hunter was booting up her laptop. 'Hang on,' he told her. 'Before you get started, I got a question: Before you called me from the motel, could they have traced you through your computer?'

'No.'

'Is that a definite no or a I-hope-not-no?'

'It's a Pentagon-DOD-NSA-Top-Secret-Clearance no.'

He looked surprised. 'You're using a National Security Agency firewall to protect your personal laptop?'

'Yep.'

'Is that legal?'

'Probably not. But since I often piddle around on it at the Store, I'd rather be safe than sorry.'

' 'Store'?'

'DOD Archives,' she explained. 'That's what everybody calls — ' She broke off and peered closer at the screen. 'I may have something . . . 'Though Senators Walsh and Cobb and Congressmen Jacobs and Stankowski disagree on almost every other issue,'' she read aloud, ''they're all adamantly opposed to human stem cell research and biological warfare.''

'That's a start,' Ben said.

'Yeah, and get this,' Hunter said, reading on, 'there's a bill about to go through Congress that would open up funding for human embryonic stem cell research and reproductive cloning — '

'Whoa. Say again for the cheap seats.'

'Reproductive cloning is the cloning of human beings . . . Incidentally, or to use your favorite word, 'coincidentally', this same bill — S-1828 — with only a few minor tweaks — was shot down in Congress two years ago by, guess who?'

'Walsh, Cobb, Jacobs and what was the other Congressman's name?'

'Stankowski. Maxwell Stankowski, a religious fundamentalist from New Jersey.'

'New Jersey? What's in New Jersey, besides Princeton and Bon Jovi?'

'Biotech Industries. Stankowski claimed they have a bunch of biochemists there who are wannabe Frankensteins. 'Course, Biotech denies it and swears all their research is strictly legal.' She paused, exhausted, and gave a terrific yawn.

Ben grinned. 'Beddy-byes for you, Ms. McCormack. Here,' he handed her the mug of hot chocolate, 'take this with you.'

'Thanks. You're sweet, but I don't drink hot chocolate. The sugar keeps me awake.'

'This isn't just hot chocolate. This is Ben's 'Special Hot Chocolate.' Try it,' he urged. 'You'll like it.' He pushed the mug to her lips.

Reluctantly, she took a sip, eyebrows arching at the taste. 'My God, how much brandy is in this?'

'To quote Gran'ma Hicks: 'Enough.'' He indicated the bathroom. 'There are towels in the cupboard under the basin. Take your pick.'

'Courtesy of Hilton or Marriott?'

'It's that obvious?'

Chuckling, she walked to the bedroom door, looked back at him and said: 'You were right, Detective Hicks.'

'About . . . ?'

'You,' she said. 'I *can* trust you.'

15

In the White House hallway leading to the James S Brady Press Room, President Evers paused to allow the make-up artist to wipe the perspiration from his face. When she was satisfied, she pulled the tissues from under his collar and stood back so he and his bustling entourage of staffers and security agents could continue walking.

At the door to the press room, Erin Scudder said: 'Now remember, Mr. President, you're just going to read a statement, so don't let the press bait you into answering questions.'

'Got it,' he said, adding: 'Hell, I wouldn't know what to tell them anyway. You've kept me so much in the dark about this — '

'It's for your own good, sir,' she reminded. 'Trust me. What you don't know can't come back and bite you in the — well, you know what I mean.'

'Ass, yeah, all too well. Nevertheless, the next free moment I get, we're going to sit down and you're going to give me some answers.'

'As you wish, Mr. President.' She flashed him a winning smile. 'Knock 'em dead, sir.'

Evers squared his big linebacker shoulders, took a deep breath and then stepped through the door. The press corps rose as he entered the room and strode up to the microphone.

'Good morning, everyone,' he said, as always lowering his voice to project strength and confidence. 'These are sad days . . . perhaps the saddest I've experienced during my stay at the White House. Joe Walsh and Mike Cobb were close personal friends of mine and, though Congressmen Jacobs and Stankowski and I were opponents in many ways, I always respected their opinions and thought highly of their integrity. They will all be sorely missed.' He paused somberly to give impact to his words, then said: 'Now, as for who's responsible for the bombing . . . the FBI assures me that it was *not* caused by terrorists. It was strictly a hate crime.

'Let me finish by saying that I have instructed the FBI to consider this investigation their top priority and to use every resource available to them. We will find these gutless murderers. We will bring them to trial. And we will see they meet the fate they so rightfully deserve. God bless you. And God bless America.'

As he gathered his speech papers and left the podium, the press started hammering him with questions, just as he'd known they would.

'Mr. President, do you think the murders are connected?'

'Does the FBI have any suspects?'

'Sir, what's your response to the white supremacist groups who claim they had no connection to the bombing?'

Erin quickly stepped between the reporters and the President. 'Sorry, boys and girls, the President isn't answering questions today.'

'Then how about *you* answering one?' said Harry Bell.

A highly respected veteran reporter for the *Washington Post*, Erin knew better than to ignore him.

'Depends what it is, Harry.'

'What about Chad, Erin? Do you have any explanation for this new virus that's only killing male refugees?'

'Sorry. No comment.'

'Thank-you-Madam-President.'

'That isn't funny, Harry. Sarcasm has been known to cost reporters their White House press passes.'

She turned and hurried after President Evers.

* * *

Ben pulled up across from the Pentagon's Metro entrance and watched, tight-lipped, as Hunter climbed out of the car. 'I'm against this, you know,' he said.

'So you keep saying.'

'Then why the hell won't you listen to me?'

''Cause I'll be fine. Ben,' she said. Then, seeing he still wasn't convinced: 'You asked me to trust you. Now I'm asking you to trust *me*. No one is going to try to kill me in the Pentagon. Fact is, I'm safer in there than I am out here.'

'Thanks.'

'Oh, for God's sake, you know I didn't mean it that way. I'm grateful for your protection. Very grateful. But if I'm going to find out what HRTM22 means, and what its connection is to all the murders, there's no better place to be than right in that very building.'

He knew she was right, but that didn't help. He watched her join a line of military and civilian personnel showing their IDs to security guards and then passing through metal detectors until she was out of sight.

This, he knew, was going to be another long day.

* * *

Hunter crossed the lobby and joined the crowd waiting in front of the elevators. She recognized several of the people. One of them, standing directly ahead of her, was General Katherinc Trilling, a woman Hunter had never met but greatly admired. Her tireless, vigorous fight for women's rights in the military, a fight that many said had hampered her career, had already reached legendary status at the Pentagon. She was also a poster girl for health, disciplined fitness and enviable beauty that, even now, in her early fifties, would have looked at home gracing the cover of *Vogue*.

One of the elevators arrived. Everyone pressed forward, filling the car. The last person to squeeze in was General Trilling. As she faced front, her cold stare settled on Hunter, now at the front of those waiting for the next car. It took a moment for recognition to sink in — and in that moment the door closed.

* * *

As soon as Hunter reached her desk, she got busy at the computer. She had access to thousands of codes, but no matter which search patterns she employed, she could find no match for HRTM22.

'Shit.'

The Key Department of Defense codes scribbled on the pad beside her were proving to be no help at all. Undaunted, she entered code after code, crossing each one off when she came up empty.

She still had a long way to go when her phone buzzed. She snatched it up irritably. 'Make it quick, Dana. I'm busy.'

The secretary's voice at the other end of the line said crisply: 'Too busy to talk to General Trilling?'

Surprised, Hunter said: 'N-No, of course not.' Then: 'Are you sure you have the right extension? This is Hunter McCormack, in cryptology.'

'How soon can you be here?' the secretary asked.

'I'm on my way,' Hunter said.

Less than five minutes later she entered General Trilling's office. The general was standing beside her desk, waiting to greet her. They shook hands, Hunter trying to match her firm grip, and then Trilling motioned for her to sit down. Hunter obeyed. General Trilling went behind her desk and sat in the uncomfortably hard straight-backed wooden chair.

'Thank you for taking the time to see me, Ms. McCormack,' she said. 'I appreciate it.'

'My pleasure, General. Oh, and congratulations on your recent promotion.'

'Thank you. I feel very honored. Women in the military have been passed over far too often when it came time for command promotions and — ' She caught herself and chuckled. 'I better not get started on that or we'll be here all day.'

Hunter smiled politely, and waited.

'I can see by your puzzled look that you're wondering why you're here.'

'It did cross my mind,' Hunter admitted. 'But, as my dad used to say: 'Everything comes to he who waits.''

General Trilling smiled, a faintly mocking smile that suggested she was merely tolerating Hunter. 'Patience is indeed a wonderful thing. Unfortunately, today it's in short supply. As a result, those who adhere to it, find themselves left behind while the rest of the world marches on.'

Hunter frowned. 'I'm not sure I understand you, General.'

'Then let me expound,' said Trilling.

* * *

Later, on her way back into the Cryptology Archives, Hunter passed the desk of her friend, Dana Petrie. Seeing she was busy, Hunter waved and kept walking.

'Hey, wait,' Dana pulled off her headset and as Hunter returned in front of her, said eagerly: 'So, what did 'General Patton' want? Details, details.'

'I don't have any.'

'Get out. You must've talked about *something*.'

'Sure. But most of it was just casual chit-chat. I tried to nail her down on some details. But she just gave me that cat-who-swallowed-the-canary smile and said that before she could discuss the project fully she wanted to get my initial response.'

''Bout what?'

'Whether I'd be interested in working in the private sector.'

'Doing what?'

'Computer forensics.'

'You're kidding! What do you know about investigating data storage devices, or analyzing sources of digital evidence?'

Hunter shrugged. 'Less than you do, apparently. But for the kind of bucks the

General said were on the table, I might be willing to learn. Besides,' she added, glancing at the end of the room, where Andy's cubicle sat painfully empty, 'I could use a change of scenery.'

'Like, to where?'

'Madison, New Jersey. General Trilling said that's where the company's headquartered.'

* * *

After Hunter had left the office, Gen. Trilling turned to the door of her adjoining bathroom and said: 'You can come out now.'

Captain Colby emerged. She'd heard the conversation between Hunter and the general and looked bleakly disappointed. 'You're calling off the dogs, ma'am?'

'Why not? Under your command, captain, a simple assassination has turned into a fucking tragi-comedy of errors.'

'General, if I may suggest — '

'You may not,' snapped General Trilling. 'What you *may* do, however, is return to your 'kennel' to await further orders.'

'General, please, give me another shot — '

'Don't argue with me, Captain. Just pray that one day I trust you enough to toss you another bone. Dismissed.'

Stung, Capt. Colby saluted and left the room.

* * *

When Hunter got off work that afternoon Ben was waiting for her in the same place he'd dropped her off that morning. The sight of him, waving to her from his blue Chevy sedan, was comforting. It assured her that no matter how much her world had been cocktail-shaken over the past forty-eight hours, she still had someone she could rely on.

As they pulled away from the curb, Ben with one eye on the rear-view mirror in case they were being tailed, she told him about her meeting with General Trilling.

He wasn't pleased. 'Jesus, you're not actually considering her offer, are you?'

'Could mean big money.'

'Big money's not going to do you any good if you're dead.' When she didn't answer, he said: 'Christ, baby, for all you know — '

Hunter cut him off. ''*Baby*'? Did you just call me *baby*?'

'Sorry, it slipped out.'

''Mean you call other women baby?'

'What the fuck has that got to do with anything?' Angry, he changed lanes and speeded up. 'In case you've forgotten, *lady*, this General Trilling character could be behind all this. You said yourself these women might be military. What if you're right? Then you'd be walking into her trap.'

'Don't have a cow,' Hunter told him. 'I'm not accepting her offer, or anyone else's right now. As for Trilling, I'm way ahead of you. This afternoon, I ditched work for an hour and tried to link her to the murdered victims.'

'And?'

'Zip. Politically, militarily and spiritually they couldn't be farther apart.'

'That still doesn't mean she — '

'Will you shut up and let me finish?'

'Sorry.'

'I did, however, uncover two interesting

facts about the General. She recently toured Central Africa — including the Sudan and Chad, where all those refugees are dying of some unknown virus — and get this; she's a silent partner at Biotech Industries.'

She expected him to react. When he didn't, she said: 'Did you hear what I said? Biotech Industries. That's in Madison — the same Madison where she said I'd be working. She could be trying to lure me there to kill me.'

Still he failed to react.

'Ben!' she snapped. 'Ben, are you listening to me?'

'Huh? Yeah, yeah.'

'What'd I just say.'

'General Trilling's a partner at Biotech.'

'Not partner. *Silent* partner.'

'She's probably just feathering her nest for when she retires. Lots of generals do that. They get elected to Boards, hire out as consultants — '

'But that's usually all done out in the open, not in secrecy.'

'Well, it can't be too secret. *You* found out about it.'

'I have the electronic resources of the free world at my fingertips. Plus, I happen to be damn good at my job.'

Ben shot her a look. 'You saying I'm not?'

'No, I — '

'Just because I got suspended doesn't mean I'm not a good detective.'

'I know that.'

'Then quit bragging, godammit.'

Stung by his harsh tone, she said: 'What's the matter?'

'Nothing.'

'Then why're you getting so pissed?'

When he didn't answer, she glanced at him. His teeth were clinched, his jaw jutted out and his hands gripped the steering-wheel so hard, his knuckles were white. She remembered then that he was an alcoholic, and guessed he was fighting his demons. 'You okay? Want me to drive?'

Ignoring her, Ben pulled over and parked outside a liquor store. Wordlessly he climbed out.

Hunter jumped out and ran after him. 'What're you doing?'

Without pausing or looking at her, he said: 'I need a drink.'

She grabbed him by the shoulder and spun him around. She barely recognized the pale, drawn, sweaty face that glared at her. But she said anyway: 'That's the last fucking thing you need.'

He gave an ugly laugh. 'Spend a lot of time counseling rummies, do you?'

'Ben, what's *wrong* with you? What the hell's going on?'

'Nothing. I just don't need some hotshot cipher-bunny telling me what I do or don't need.'

His words cut deep. 'Then I'll make it easy for you,' she said. Reaching into the car, she grabbed her purse and computer case and stormed off.

Ben watched her go. Angry and frustrated with himself, he wasn't sure if she was really leaving or just trying to provoke him into action.

Either way, it didn't matter. He had no other choice. He had to enter that liquor store.

16

Hunter walked to the end of the block, emotions churning out of control. She felt Ben had betrayed her; that protecting her was only important when he didn't need a drink. At the same time she knew that he was sick and needed help and understanding, not a fairweather friend who took off the minute it started raining.

But most of all, she felt a deep and wholly unexpected sense of loss that they were no longer together. She tried to kid herself that what she felt for him was only sympathy; the same kind of sympathy he'd originally felt for her. He'd felt sorry for her and now she felt sorry for him. That was all. Nothing more. Now they were even.

But deep down, where you can't lie to yourself, she knew that wasn't it at all. What she felt for Ben wasn't sympathy. She actually cared about him; liked having him around; felt safe with him.

Admittedly he was a drunk and that saddened and disappointed her. But he was genuine. What you saw was what you got. And there weren't too many of those men left in the world: not in *her* world, anyway.

As her anger faded, she slowed her pace. Her conscience told her that she'd been wrong to run out on him. She should have been bigger than that; more compassionate. But it was too late now. By now he would have already bought a bottle of J.D. and was probably parked in a dark, empty alley somewhere, drinking himself into oblivion.

She tried to imagine how he must be feeling; how alone he must be, his eyes so haunted, his soul filled with despair as he tried to block out whatever pain it was that had caused him to drink in the first place. She wondered what that pain was: a woman, maybe? A shooting that somehow went awry? A stray, ricocheting bullet that fate decided should take the life an innocent bystander? As a cop, he faced death and tragedy and human nature at its worst on a daily basis. *My*

God, who wouldn't need a drink?

Anger gone and ashamed of her lack of empathy, she decided to go back and try to help Ben fight his demons. Stopping, she turned around — and immediately collided with someone who'd been walking directly behind her.

She started to apologize and then stopped, surprised, as she felt something hard jam into her side. She knew instantly that it was a gun and froze.

'Keep walking,' Lieutenant Chavez said softly. Then, when Hunter didn't move: 'Make a scene, bitch, and I'll take you out right here.'

She dug her silenced 9mm harder into Hunter's ribs.

Numbly, Hunter slowly started walking. Lieutenant Chavez walked beside her, the raincoat folded over her arm hiding the gun buried in Hunter's side.

Just ahead, an alley divided an all-night convenience store from a takeout pizza joint. Hunter, knowing she was dead once they were in the alley, desperately tried to think of a way to escape. Trying to run away would be suicide; and guessing this redhead was connected to the woman who'd ruthlessly killed Andy, Hunter had no illusions of trying to bargain for her life. But what other option was there?

They reached the alley.

Hunter stopped and immediately felt the gun prod her into its shadows.

'Keep going,' Chavez hissed.

Hunter hesitated for another moment — and in that moment there was a blur of motion behind them as someone slammed into Chavez, sending her sprawling. Hunter felt herself pulled roughly aside by the same someone who then stepped in front of her. She saw it was Ben, a stone-cold sober Ben with a snub-nosed .38 in his fist, but for an instant doubted her eyes.

'Get behind me,' he yelled. Not waiting to see if she obeyed, he turned back to Lieutenant Chavez, who, now on her hands and knees, was scrambling to retrieve her weapon.

'Bad idea,' Ben said.

Chavez stopped, hand only inches from her dropped weapon.

'Well, if it ain't the fucking cavalry,' she said, and finally made her move.

Ben shot her in the forehead.

Lieutenant Chavez fell backward, eyes full of disbelief and hate, and collapsed, dead.

'C'mon,' Ben told Hunter. 'Let's go!'

Still shaken by his sudden appearance, she didn't move.

Then a passerby saw the corpse, the blood welling from the hole in its forehead, and screamed.

The scream jarred Hunter back to reality. She looked about her. Alerted by the scream, other pedestrians were stopping, staring, pointing at the dead woman.

Ben grabbed Hunter's arm, 'Let's go!' and dragged her to his car, idling at the curb behind them. Pushing her into the passenger-seat, he ran around and jumped in behind the wheel. Then, gunning the gas, he burned rubber as he drove off and became part of the late-night traffic.

They didn't speak for several blocks. Shortly, Ben and the cars around him pulled over as an ambulance raced past them, headed in the other direction. Its blaring siren blended in with the sirens of two police cars that were following it.

Once they were moving again, Ben turned down a sidestreet. There was no traffic and only a few pedestrians. Ben slowed down, turned to Hunter and asked her if she was okay.

Fear still controlled her voice, so she nodded.

'Lucky I recognized the Camry,' Ben said. 'Otherwise, I wouldn't have been able to spring the trap.'

'Trap?' She frowned, confused. 'What're you talking about?'

'The night Andy was killed, he and the person I thought was his lover got out of a metallic-silver Camry. I caught a glimpse of it behind us as we were driving here.'

'But this isn't the woman who killed Andy.'

'Maybe not. But it's the same car. I remembered the license plate.'

Recalling how disinterested he'd been when she mentioned General Trilling's involvement in Biotech Industries, Hunter said: 'I'm confused. Are you saying you knew she was tailing us all the time?'

'No, not until I saw the Camry and remembered the plate. Well, actually I only remembered the first three letters. That's why I ducked into that liquor store — so I could watch and see if she pulled over. Once she did, I knew — '

Hunter had heard enough. 'You bastard!' she erupted. 'You lousy, fucking bastard! You used me as bait!'

'Whoa, calm down. I had no choice,' Ben said.

'You risked my fucking life, you sonofabitch, just so you could get to her.'

'Well, I had to be sure and — ' He broke off as she started punching him. The car swerved dangerously as he tried to protect himself from her flurry of wild blows. 'Whoa, whoa . . . calm down . . . '

The attack ended as suddenly as it had started. Drained, Hunter slumped against the door, her chest heaving from exertion.

'Easy,' Ben said, 'easy.'

'Fuck you and your easy.'

'Look, I'm sorry. I never would have let anything happen to you. You know that.'

'I don't know anything. I trusted you, you sonofabitch — trusted you with my fucking life and . . . and then you pull this kind of shit.'

He shrugged, momentarily doubting himself. 'Maybe you're right. Maybe I was wrong to do it. Maybe I should've clued you in. I don't know. All I knew was these were ruthless, cold-blooded killers we were dealing with, no-good bastards who killed without any qualms or conscience. And knowing that, I wanted to make sure the shooter thought we were separated before — '

' — she tried to shoot me?'

'I would never have let that happen. Surely you know that by now. I just wanted to question her, find out what's really going on. I didn't plan to kill her.'

They turned down another street. It was dark and quiet and Ben pulled over and cut the engine.

'Please believe that, Hunter.'

'Why? So you can set me up again?'

Stung, he pulled the keys from the ignition and dropped them in her lap. He then got out, slammed the door and walked off.

Hunter sat there a moment, cheeks wet with angry tears. Then, knowing she couldn't let him walk out of her life, she scrambled over behind the wheel, fired up the engine, and put the car into reverse.

She quickly caught up with him. He was still in the street, walking alongside the parked cars. She braked and lowered the passenger-side window.

'Ben, wait — '

He ignored her; kept walking.

She continued to back up, keeping abreast of him, saying: 'Ben — Ben, listen to me. I'm sorry for what I said. But good Christ, Ben, you should've told me. Should've let me know what you were doing instead of pretending you needed a drink.'

He smiled sourly. 'Who says I was pretending?' He held up his hands to her. They were shaking. 'Right now I'd *Kill* for a drink.'

'Killing isn't something I'd bring up right now.'

'Sorry. Bad choice of words. But I really could use some J.D.' He exaggerated his shaking and despite herself she gave a tiny smile.

'Forgive me?' he asked.

'No.'

'Aww, c'mon. I did save your life.'

'Only after you endangered it in the first place.'

'I'm serious, baby. Forgive me?'

'On one condition.'

'Name it.'

'You stop calling me baby.'

⋆ ⋆ ⋆

Later that night, across town in her silent, austere bedroom, General Trilling sat in bed drinking sixty-year-old cognac while reading military briefs. *CNN News* was on television, the sound muted.

Graphic shots of male corpses being dumped in a mass grave in the desert outside Camp Geneva filled the screen.

General Trilling occasionally glanced at the TV, her cold expression showing no regard for the inexplicable tragedy, and then went back to her briefs. She was reading the last one when there was a soft knock on her door. 'Come in, Jill.'

The door opened and Lieutenant Avery entered. She stood at attention at the foot of the bed until General Trilling finished reading and looked up.

'Yes?'

'I'm sorry to bother you so late, ma'am, but Lieutenant Chavez has been killed.'

General Trilling displayed no emotion. 'Positive ID?'

'Yes, ma'am. One round in the forehead. Shooter unknown.'

'Location?'

'Downtown D.C.. I'm getting other specifics as we speak.'

General Trilling thought a moment. 'Killed in the line of duty,' she murmured. 'Well, there's no better way to go. Thank you, Jill. Good night.'

'Good night, ma'am.' Avery saluted smartly and marched out.

General Trilling stared at the TV as if it were the enemy. *Hunter McCormack*, she thought without rancor, *you must have nine lives*.

17

Ben was unable to sleep that night. The red digital numbers displayed on the cable box clock under the TV seemed to be changing in slow motion. Minutes lasted hours, it seemed. Finally, shortly after three, Ben got up off the couch, padded into the kitchen and turned on the coffeemaker. As he sat on one of the counter stools, waiting for the coffee to brew, he let his mind drift back to what had happened earlier.

When he and Hunter finally got back to the apartment, he'd fixed two Denver omelettes while she showered. Neither spoke much as they ate — talking seemed superfluous after what they'd been through. Besides, though Hunter was safe for the moment, both understood that the enemy was powerful and had impressive resources at its disposal. No matter where she went, or how hard she tried to hide, sooner or later they'd track her down and again try to kill her. It was a chilling thought. It made them realize that in order for her — maybe both of them — to remain alive, they had to stay one step ahead of the killers. And to do that Hunter either had to turn to the FBI for help and hope that they believed her story and agreed to protect her — which was unlikely, since she had no proof that General Trilling was behind the attempts on her life — or try to find out as much about her as possible and then use that information to their advantage.

Now, as Ben thought about the latter option, he heard the bedroom door open. He turned and saw Hunter standing in the doorway. She yawned, barely awake, and rubbed her eyes with one fist. Her hair was a mess, she wore no makeup and was naked under his old Washington Redskins jersey . . . and Ben knew he'd never seen a more desirable woman in his life.

'I heard a noise,' she said.

'It's just me,' he said. 'Go back to bed.'

She yawned and studied him with sleep-filled eyes. 'Coffee?'

'Sure.' He found another cup and filled

it, and his own from the coffee maker.

Hunter sat on the stool beside him. For a few moments neither spoke as they sipped their coffee. Then she indicated the photograph of Marcus, Janelle and their four year-old daughter, Jasmine. 'Nice-looking family.'

Ben nodded, and tried to hide the pain he always felt whenever he looked at the photograph.

Hunter peered closer at Janelle. 'She looks familiar.'

Swallowing hard, he said, 'She's a newscaster on one of the local stations.'

'Oh sure, Janelle Freeman. She's good.' Gesturing to Marcus she added playfully, 'He could put his shoes under my bed any day.'

'We graduated from the Academy together,' Ben said, and for the first time she became aware of just how flat and mechanical his voice had become. 'Used to be partners.'

'How come you ended up with that other guy, Harper?'

'Because Marcus was killed. Thanks to me.'

There was nothing she could say to that. And even if there had been, she doubted if Ben would have heard it. The way he was staring into the steam rising from his coffee . . . she knew he was someplace else.

'Two years ago,' he said in a soft, dead voice, 'we were involved in a high speed pursuit. A tire blew and I lost control of the car. I broke my nose. Marcus broke his *neck*.'

Sensing that this pain was the thing that was eating away at him, she gently pressed her hand over his. 'Come to bed,' she said.

But he was still looking back at the past.

'When Andy was killed,' she reminded, 'you told me not to blame myself. You might want to consider your own advice.'

He showed no sign of hearing her.

Hunter took her coffee into the living room and turned on the TV. 'Ben!' she called. 'Come and take a look at this!'

The urgency in her voice jerked him out of his reverie. Rising, he entered the living room and saw that she was watching one of the twenty-four hour news stations. It was covering some kind of protest.

'That's Biotech, isn't it?' he said.

Hunter nodded.

On-screen protesters were trying to tear down a chain-link fence that surrounded the property. Baton-wielding security guards and dog handlers were struggling to drive them back.

'They're threatening to bomb the lab if they don't stop cloning,' said Hunter. 'Do you really think they would?'

'Wouldn't be the first time. Back in the fifties, when my Grampa was in Naval Intelligence, he swore up and down that joint Army-Navy-CIA experiments were conducted in New York and San Francisco, exposing tens of thousands of people to airborne germs.'

'I never heard anything about that.'

'The public wasn't meant to. But years later, when people in those cities began getting ill from strange viruses that caused cancer there was such a furore that protesters tried to destroy the labs that produced the chemicals and — '

Suddenly Hunter was wide awake. 'What did you say?'

'Protesters tried to destroy — '

'No, before that. About strange viruses that caused cancer?'

'That's what they claimed. No one could prove it, of course. By then the government had covered it up. Just like they covered up the rumors at Fort Detrick.'

'What rumors?'

'I don't remember all the details. It was back in the mid-70s and I was more interested in football than Grampa's anti-government rhetoric. But it had to do with Congress granting funding for a synthetic biological agent that produced AIDS-like retroviruses.'

'Christ.'

'That was followed by a special virus program, purportedly to develop cancer-causing viruses. When word leaked out what was going on, there was a national outcry. Funding was suspended and the name of the program was changed.'

Hunter leapt up off the sofa and disappeared into the bedroom. When she returned she was carrying her laptop.

Setting it on the coffee table, she booted it up and then typed in a search term. A few moments later they were both hunched together over the screen, reading a newspaper article from 1975.

* * *

Fort Detrick, Maryland. The virus section of Fort Detrick's Center for Biological Warfare Research has been renamed the Frederick Cancer Research Facilities, supervised by the National Cancer Institute (NCI).

* * *

'I guess Grampa wasn't so far off-base after all,' muttered Ben.

Hunter was still reading. She stiffened when she reached a telling paragraph. 'Listen to this. 'Eventually, retrovirologists isolated a virus to which no immunity exists. It was later renamed HTLV, Human T-cell Leukemia Virus, in order for Congress to pass a bill justifying billions in government funding.''

She looked up at him as something struck her.

'What?' Ben asked.

'I've been looking in the wrong place.'

She typed furiously for a moment. Ben watched as an alphabet appeared, with the numbers 1 to 26 below each letter. Hunter highlighted M (13) and T (20). The pitch of her voice betraying her excitement, she said, 'HRTM22 isn't a code, Ben. It's a *bill!*'

'You've lost me.'

'Thirteen and twenty equals thirty three,' she explained. 'And H period R period, followed by a dash, stands for the House of Representatives.'

'H.R.-3322?'

'Exactly.'

'So why didn't Teri just write 3322?'

'Why does anybody use a code? To disguise whatever message they're sending.' Thinking of Teri made her deflate suddenly. 'Didn't do her much good, though, did it? They still killed her.'

'That's in the past, Hunter, and there's no changing it. But it could be that we're getting closer to her killers.' He nodded at the laptop. 'What else have you got?'

She thought for a moment, then clicked one of her desktop icons, launching a program called *GovTrack.us*.

He watched as she scrolled through a seemingly endless list of past proposed legislation. Each bill was numbered and preceded by either *H* for House or *S* For Senate, and followed by the date and time it was passed or debated.

Forty minutes later she'd gone back three years but still hadn't found H.R.-3322. 'Christ,' she said, 'I can't believe how much of this stuff never gets past debate.'

'Welcome to The Hill,' Ben said. Then, as she yawned: 'Want me take over for a while?'

'I could use a pee break.'

'Well, never let it be said that I interfered with the call of nature.'

Hunter rose and stretched the stiffness out of her muscles. 'Do you know what you're looking for?'

'Woman, I resent your tone. It implies I am not capable of the task — wait, here it is! Uh-oh.'

'What?'

'I'm being blocked. It's telling me that H.R.-3322 'requires special access.''

'That's impossible.'

'See for yourself.'

Hunter, her bathroom break temporarily forgotten, sat down and typed rapidly, then cursed when she received the same message. She continued typing, but the blocking message persisted. 'Dammit, what the hell's going on? No one can restrict a bill. All legislature records are open to inspection at all times.'

'Obviously someone begs to differ.'

'Yeah, well, I can soon fix that. Feel like taking a drive?'

'Where to?'

'The Pentagon.'

* * *

The silvery promise of a new day streaked the eastern horizon as Ben pulled up outside the Pentagon's south parking lot and let Hunter out.

'Call me the moment you know something,' he said. 'And remember, only use the cell I gave you. That way no one can trace you.'

'Got it. Meanwhile, you scoot over to the Library of Congress. The Jefferson Building opens at 8:30. Give this to Brian in the Computer Catalogue Center.' She handed Ben a note. 'He'll get you what you need.'

'*You're* what I need.'

'A romantic cop,' she said, twinkling. 'Just my luck.' Impulsively she kissed him and walked away.

Ben glanced down at the note and frowned. 'Hey!'

'What?'

'What the hell is the *United States Pharmacopeia?*'

'A compendium of quality control tests for drugs and excipients to be introduced into a medicinal formulation.'

'Ah,' said Ben wryly. 'That explains it nicely.'

He watched as Security checked her ID and passed her on through. Then with a sigh of concern, he drove off.

* * *

Hunter stepped out of the elevator onto the subbasement level and showed her security clearance to the guard, who waved her through. She walked the length of the corridor, knowing that security cameras were monitoring her every move. She tried to appear casual, as if this were no big thing, merely another day at the office.

She reached the door of room 2SB197, swiped her card through the lock and entered. With the door closed, she sat at the computer and logged on. Recognizing her security codes, the screen lit up. She was in.

She typed: CONGRESSIONAL RESEARCH SERVICE.

A window marked TRACK CONGRESS opened up.

SEARCH BY BILL NUMBER.

She tapped in H.R.-3322 and pressed *Enter*.

Almost immediately H.R.-3322 appeared on the screen. Hunter typed *Open*. But equally fast the message RESTRICTED. NO ACCESS appeared on the screen.

Hunter scowled. *Okay*, she thought.

Let the games begin . . .

She typed in a series of overriding codes, but received the same response every time. Irked, she continued to try other codes in hopes of bypassing the firewall blocking unauthorized access.

This was going to be a challenge.

* * *

General Trilling was asleep when the bedside phone rang. She rolled over, yawned, and answered it: 'Speak.'

A voice at the other end of the line said: 'Ma'am, this is Major Trask. You asked to be notified if anyone attempted to access H.R.-3322.'

She tensed. 'Has our firewall been breached?'

'No, General. Only someone with Pentagon or NSA top level over-ride codes could penetrate our security.'

'Thank you, Major. I appreciate the heads-up. Good night.' Ending the call, she glanced at the bedside clock. It read 5:21 AM. She called her aide, said: 'Jill, get my car ready. And call Captain Colby.

Have her assemble the squad.'
'Yes, ma'am.'
Trilling hung up, then called another number. It rang a few times, and then Erin Scudder's sleepy voice answered: 'What is it?'
'It's Katherine. I need you to act upon something immediately.'

⋆ ⋆ ⋆

It took a while and all her code expertise, but Hunter finally gained access to H.R.-3322. Feeling a sense of triumph, she hit *Print*. As page after page began to spew out of the printer, she got up and stretched.
When the printout was finished, she gathered the pages together. Then, pulling up her shirt, she taped them around her waist, tucked her shirt back in and left the room.

⋆ ⋆ ⋆

General Trilling's car stopped outside a disused warehouse. Two black SUVs were already parked at the curb, waiting for her. Trilling climbed out and marched along the sidewalk until she reached Captain Colby and a ten-woman squad, all of whom were dressed in military fatigues and standing at attention. 'I want every exit of the Pentagon covered,' she told Colby. 'McCormack must not get away.'

'Does the General want her alive or dead?'

'Dead,' Trilling said without hesitation. 'But not on government property.'

'Yes, ma'am.'

'Don't screw up again, Captain. There's been enough of that already. I'll be at Biotech,' she added. 'Call me the minute it's done.'

* * *

In his private quarters at the White House, President Evers studied the photograph Scudder had just given him. 'And this is the woman who claimed she saw someone deliberately drown Joe Walsh?'

Scudder nodded. 'But we now have reason to believe that she was the actual killer. We also have reason to believe she's smuggled highly classified documents out of the Pentagon.'

'Who's behind it? The Russians or the Chinese?'

'We don't know that yet, Mr. President. But we do know that her accomplice is a suspended Homicide detective named Ben Hicks.'

Evers swore softly. 'A cop? Sonofabitch! Doesn't anyone have a sense of patriotism anymore?' He looked at Scudder. 'I assume you've notified the FBI?'

'Sir, I didn't think the Administration needed another hit right now.'

'Meaning?'

'I thought you'd want 'our people' to handle things. But if you'd prefer, I can bring in the FBI and risk having this leaked to the networks.'

'No, no. The last thing I need is an espionage scandal. I already have enough problems with this hate bombing. You made the right call, Erin.'

'Thank you, Mr. President.'

She turned and left the room. His praise made her glow.

18

As the Pentagon elevator rose toward the lobby, Hunter speed-dialed a number on her cell phone. 'Hi. I need a cab to pick me up at the entrance to the south parking lot of the Pentagon . . . I know they won't let him in. Tell the driver I'll meet him outside the gate.'

⋆ ⋆ ⋆

Six of Captain Colby's paramilitary squad positioned themselves around the Pentagon Metro entrances so that they could monitor everyone who came and went. At the same time, Captain Colby's SUV pulled up to the South Entrance parking lot. She and the remainder of her contingent showed their IDs to Gate Security, who passed them through.

⋆ ⋆ ⋆

In the lobby, Hunter waited while a Pentagon security guard checked the contents of her purse and then allowed her to exit the building.

Outside the day had dawned bright and clear. Hunter put on her sunglasses and started across the parking lot toward the gate. After a few steps she paused as she spotted the blonde who'd killed Andy, leading four women in military fatigues toward the building. Alarmed, Hunter ducked behind a row of parked cars. From here, she watched as Colby and her squad marched past.

They didn't see her, and as soon as they'd passed Hunter ran to the gate.

Captain Colby and her squad had almost reached the entrance to the Pentagon when one of the women spotted Hunter. 'Captain!' she said, pointing. 'There she is!'

* * *

Hunter reached the parking lot gate and looked around for her cab. It wasn't there. Trying not to panic, she walked through the gate. Looking back, she saw Captain Colby and her squad sprinting toward her. They were still seventy-five yards away. Hunter again looked around for the cab.

Nothing.

Her pursuers were now no more than fifty yards away.

Still no cab.

Her pursuers were now less than forty yards away and closing fast.

Hunter knew she couldn't wait much longer. She was about to run when a Yellow Cab pulled up. She yanked open the door and squeezed inside. 'Library of Congress,' she told the driver. 'And there's an extra twenty in it if you hurry!'

He nodded, burning rubber as he drove off.

* * *

As the cab pulled away, Colby slowed her pace and swore under her breath. Knowing how General Trilling would react if Hunter escaped, she memorized the license plate and got out her cell phone, punched in a number and said: 'All of you — get back here on the double!'

* * *

Hunter found Ben hunched over a computer in the Library of Congress Jefferson Building reading room. Two boxes of CDs lay nearby, the first labeled *United States Pharmacopeia*, the second *The International Pharmacopoeia*. One look at Ben's tired eyes and disheveled hair told her that it had been a long morning.

'How's it going?' she asked, sitting beside him.

'It isn't. There's a ton of cancer-causing drugs and excipients listed, but none linked to either the U.S. military or Biotech Industries.'

'I'm not surprised. Proves that whoever is behind the virus wanted no one to know about it. But it won't help them.' She set the printout of H.R.-3322 on the table before him. 'We have them by the short 'n' curlies, as my dad used to say.'

* * *

Gary Bennett, dispatcher at the Yellow Cab Company on Bladensburg Road NE, ended the call and looked down at the hard-faced blonde behind the wheel of the black SUV. She'd parked in the entrance, and refused to move until he answered her question. There were four paramilitary types in the vehicle with her; another six in the SUV behind them. Though they were all women, they looked capable of killing anyone who defied them and deciding he didn't need any more grief than he already had, he checked his logbook, said: 'My driver dropped her off at the Library of Congress. Jefferson Building. Now, can I *please* have my garage back?'

* * *

Ben scanned the printout and started skip-reading: ' ' . . . to promote the health of the Armed Forces and their dependents by enhancing cancer research and treatment, blah, blah, blah . . . to provide for a study of the epidemiological causes of cancer among various ethnic groups . . . and related Agencies, Appropriation Act, 2007 . . . ' Jesus! How many palms were greased to get this through Congress?'

'About the same number of blind eyes that were turned in order to overlook all the amendments that allowed the funding to go to just about anyone with their hand out,' said Hunter. She found herself studying his profile, enjoying the feeling of reassurance she got whenever he was around. 'Like you said: Welcome to The Hill.'

'Okay, so we're on a roll. What's the connection between the military sneaking a bill through Congress three years ago so they could improve their germ warfare program and the murder of two Senators and two Congressmen opposed to human embryonic stem cell research?'

'I'm still trying to figure that out.'

'And?'

'So far zilch. Separately, they make sense — well, not sense, because the idea of a government creating a cancer-causing virus so they can wipe out their enemies is pure insanity in the first place — but at least it gives us a reason. And murdering politicians opposed to your bill, a bill that's going to net someone like Biotech Industries billions . . . well, again there's a certain logic to it. But put the two together and . . . '

Ben gave the matter a moment's thought. 'What if they aren't connected?'

'More coincidence? I can't buy that.'

'Me, either.' He paused, then said: 'Okay. What if the connection is less obvious?'

'Go on.'

'What if it's somehow linked to the murder of your friend in Baltimore?'

'Teri?'

'Why not? I mean, we know why they're after you. You saw Senator Walsh murdered. And Andy, well, poor devil, he was just in the wrong place at the wrong — '

'No, no. He was killed because, according to the shooter, they thought he knew about H.R.-3322.'

'Could Teri have been killed for the same reason? We know she knew about it because she texted you.'

'But you said a burglar killed her.'

'That's what we assumed at the time. But now, with all this other shit going on, we have to consider other options — like, someone staging the robbery to cover up her murder.'

Struck by something, Hunter whispered a name.

'What was that?' he asked.

'*Utopians*,' she said.

'Who?'

'Teri belonged to a group called the Utopians. She mentioned it in an earlier email. Said they were all high-profile women — doctors, lawyers, scientists, politicians, I think she even said generals — '

'The kind of general who might say 'drain the swamp' and be referring to 'mosquitoes' as far away as Chad?'

Hunter felt a cold lump form in her stomach. They were onto something. They were really onto something. 'Something else that fits,' she muttered. 'Teri said these women intend to wipe out all the militants of the world and are willing to go to any extreme to achieve their goal.'

'Keep going.'

'What if they're experimenting with a new form of cancer warfare? Most militants are men, and the only refugees dying in Chad are males, remember?'

'Okay. Let's say we're right about this, that the Utopians intend to kill off all the bad guys in the world by giving them an incurable cancer — which, by the way, some people might not think is a bad idea. How do we tie all the facts together so we can get someone important to not only believe us, but also be willing to help us? I mean, up until a few days ago, *I* would've called you crazy. In fact, I'd probably think you were less crazy if you told me you'd been abducted by little green men.'

'If you're right about this, we need to get a list of all the members.'

'Maybe they have a website.'

He sat back and gestured to the keyboard. 'So what arc you waiting for?'

She shrugged. 'We'd better get out of here first. Go back to your apartment.'

He frowned. 'Why?'

'That blonde who killed Andy? I ran into her and a squad of armed women this morning, at the Pentagon.'

'Jesus. Did she see you?'

'Yes.'

She explained what had happened.

'Jesus,' Ben said. 'How come you didn't tell me this before?'

'I figured you had enough on your plate.'

'Well, next time let me decide, okay?' Rising, he added: 'C'mon. Let's get out of here.'

They left the reading room but didn't take the elevator. Ben led them down the fire stairs until they came to the lobby. He peered through the window. It was crowded, but there was no sight of the blonde or her armed squad.

'Let's go.'

They pushed out into the foyer with Ben leading the way, just as Captain Colby and her squad entered. Ben stopped, turned and pushed Hunter back toward the stairs. 'It's them!'

'How the hell did they know I was here?'

'I don't know and there isn't time to find out.'

Ben led the way to the stairs. Pushing through the double-swing-doors, he paused and looked through the window.

Colby and four of her squad were elbowing their way through the crowd toward them. The others were watching the exit.

'Shit. C'mon . . . '

Opening the door to the stairs, he followed Hunter down to the basement. There, beyond another door, was a security station manned by a Library of Congress security guard. Before him stood a line of visitors, all waiting to have their passes checked.

'Now what?' Ben hissed.

Hunter's only response was to march up to the front of the line and flash her ID at the guard. 'I'm Hunter McCormack with the NSA, and this is Detective Hicks. Congressman Delano is expecting us.'

The guard reached for the phone. 'I'll tell his office you're here.'

'We can't wait for a staffer to come

down and get us,' Hunter said impatiently. 'This is an emergency. Just call the Congressman and tell him we're on our way!'

Reading uncertainty in the guard's expression, Ben said: 'You heard her! Do it! *Now!*'

They pushed on through the doors.

'Wait!' yelled the guard. 'You gotta be accompanied by — '

He got no further. The people standing in line began demanding to also be let through.

The guard hesitated, torn between going after Hunter and Ben and doing his job before mutiny broke out in the line. 'I'm sorry,' he told them. 'But rules are rules. I can't let you in there without an escort.'

Hunter and Ben sprinted along the lighted tunnel leading to the street. 'Where the hell are we going?' he asked breathlessly.

'You don't know?' she said, surprised. 'The Cannon Building.'

Ben shook his head. 'I've got to get out more often.'

* * *

Captain Colby and her squad moved to the head of the line. She thrust a photograph of Hunter into the security guard's face. 'This woman,' she barked. 'Was she here?'

'First,' the guard said, 'show me some ID.'

'I'm on official military business,' she lied.

'I don't doubt that, Captain. But I still can't let you pass without a staffer escorting you.'

It would have been so easy to break his neck. He'd be dead before he knew it. But not here, not now, in front of witnesses. Frustrated, Captain Colby turned and motioning for her squad to follow, hurried back the way they'd come.

19

When Hunter and Ben entered the Cannon Building they spotted another security checkpoint, this one including a metal detector. Ben stopped to get his wind, and indicating his ankle holster said: 'Be nice to have a Plan B right about now.'

Hunter thought on her feet. 'We do.'

'We do?'

'We rehearsed it in the diner, remember?'

Ben frowned, wondering what she was referring to. Then it hit him. 'Ohhh, the *diner*,' he said. 'Yeah, sure . . . '

He took out his gun, released the safety and handed it to her.

Holding the gun by finger and thumb, as if she were afraid it might come to life and bite her, Hunter approached the guard.

'Officer . . . officer . . . I found this in the tunnel.'

The guard threw her a disinterested glance — until he spotted the weapon.

Then he thrust out his left hand and grabbed the grips of his own gun. 'Hold it, lady! Stay right where you are!'

Ignoring him, Hunter said innocently, 'I thought it was a toy, but now I'm not so sure.'

The people around her started to scatter.

'Put the gun down, lady. Now!'

Ben hurried up behind her. 'Do as he says, baby. Please . . . '

Hunter looked at him. 'Oh, all right. Here, officer.'

She dropped the gun and it went off as it hit the marble floor.

The sound was emphasized by the confines of the building, and the angry whine of the ricocheting bullet panicked everyone.

Ben and Hunter slipped away in the chaos.

* * *

They burst out of the building and quickly lost themselves among the passersby. Ben looked back and saw the blonde and her squad come out of the Madison Building and hurry across the street to the Cannon Building. Cars had to stop or swerve to avoid hitting them. Drivers angrily hit their horns.

Hunter and Ben took the first left and kept walking until they reached Ben's sedan. While Hunter jumped in, Ben tore a ticket from the windshield and checked his watch.

'Goddammit! Can you believe this shit? The meter's barely expired!'

Hunter glared at him. 'Keep talking and *we'll* be expired.'

He got in beside her, gunned the engine and peeled away from the curb. After a minute or so he grinned and said, 'We make a good team, baby.'

She let that one go. 'I'm sorry about your gun.'

'I can always get another. Besides, we have bigger problems. We have to find somebody we can trust. We turn over something as explosive as this to the wrong person and one way or another we'll get buried.'

'You think it goes all the way to the top?'

'I hate to think so. I voted for the guy.'

'Me, too. Don't you know anybody important who you can trust?'

'I used to know a guy who wrote obits for the *Post*, but he died.' He fell silent for a moment, then said: 'What about the NSA? Surely your boss would help us out?'

'My boss is a woman,' Hunter replied meaningfully. 'A very driven woman who doesn't have a high regard for men *or* militants. I wouldn't put it past her to be one of the Utopians.' Suddenly she turned and looked at him. 'Wait a minute . . . you *do* know somebody: that newscaster — Janelle Freeman. A story like this would send her ratings through the roof.'

When he didn't reply, she said: 'Well, don't die of enthusiasm.'

Ben said: 'It's a great idea.'

'But you hate it?'

'I love it. Trouble is, I haven't spoken to Janelle since the funeral.'

'Now,' she told him, 'might be a good time to start.'

* * *

Janelle lived in a modest home on a tree-lined street. Ben pulled up across from it but made no attempt to get out.

'Look,' Hunter said. 'If you really don't think she'll help us then let's not go through with this.'

Ben gave a tight, mirthless grin. 'That's not what's bothering me. I'm just trying to think of what I'll say when she asks me where the fuck I've been all this time.' He shrugged. 'What the hell. Maybe she won't even be home.'

They got out and walked up the path to the door. Ben brushed himself down, trying not to look like the wreck he was. He rang the bell, waited. A moment later the door opened and a pretty child of seven or eight looked up at them.

Ben swallowed and forced a smile. 'Hi, Jasmine. Remember me?'

She stared up at him but said nothing, and her large dark eyes gave nothing away.

From inside the house Janelle called: 'Who is it, honey?'

Jasmine hesitated before saying: 'Uncle Ben.'

There was a long pause. Then: 'Who?'

A moment later Janelle joined them. She looked more shocked than angry to see him.

'Hello, Janelle,' he said quietly.

'B-Ben . . . what're you doing here?'

'We need your help.'

She hadn't been expecting that, but it didn't change her reaction at all. 'Sorry,' she said, and without another word, she closed the door.

Ben looked at Hunter and shrugged, then turned and walked back to the car. Hunter followed him, looking at the defeated slope of his shoulders. 'Don't worry,' she said. 'It was worth a try.'

'Where does that leave us now?'

'Ever heard of Shit Creek?'

He grinned ruefully. 'Just off Diarrhea Drive, as I recall. It's where I've lived most of my life.'

They got back in the car. Ben made a U-turn and started back toward the city. He hadn't gone far when he noticed something in his rear-view mirror — Jasmine, pedaling like crazy to catch up with them.

He pulled over and waited for her to

draw level with them. 'What is it, Jas'?'

'Mommy says to wait for her at Starbucks.'

'Which one?'

Jasmine pointed ahead. 'It's in the mini-mall two blocks up.'

Impulsively he leaned out the window and kissed her on the cheek. 'See you soon, sweetheart.'

When Janelle finally joined them, Hunter politely excused herself and went to the restroom.

'Can I get you something?' Ben asked Janelle.

'Thanks. I can only stay a minute.'

There was a brief, awkward silence between them. He wanted to say so much, but now that he had the chance, words failed him.

'I'm sorry I couldn't invite you in,' she said at last, 'but my dad's living with us now, and . . . you know how he feels about you.'

'Yeah. Can't say as I blame him.'

'No, he's wrong, Ben. He's my dad and I love him dearly, but . . . he's wrong. I read the reports. No one said you'd been drinking. If they had, I wouldn't be talking to you now.'

Unable to meet her direct gaze, unable for the moment to speak, he looked down at his lap and nodded.

'But I *am* angry at you for abandoning us. I needed you. So did Jasmine. You should have been there for us.'

'I know that. And I have no excuse. What's worse: in my shoes Marcus would have been there for you.' He drew a breath. 'If it's not too late, I'd like to sign up from now on.'

'I'd like that. So would Jasmine. But first I'll have to work on my dad. He's not well and I'll have to go at him slowly. Fair enough?'

'More than fair.'

'Okay. Now — how can I help you?'

* * *

In Janelle's office at WRJA-TV, Ben and Hunter studied the pages Hunter had just printed out on Janelle's printer. Under a website heading, *The Utopians*, was a list of names headed by General Katherine

Trilling. Among the other prominent members was Erin Scudder, Chief of Staff at the White House.

Ben gave a low whistle. 'This is a game-winning touchdown.'

'Or a pair of Jimmy Choo shoes.'

The door opened and Janelle said: 'We're on.'

Karl Smanski, her producer, read everything through twice and then looked at Hunter and Ben. His office was filled with Emmys and other broadcasting awards. After a moment he said: 'I wonder if you have any idea how this is going to affect your lives?'

'You make it sound ominous.'

'Could be.'

He picked up one of the phones on his desk and said: 'Arlene, get me Dennis DeWitt's office.' He gave them another look. 'He's the White House Press Secretary.'

* * *

Just down the hall from the Oval Office, Dennis DeWitt sat at his desk, phone against his ear as he scribbled notes on a pad. The information he'd just received turned his blood cold. Finished writing, he said into the phone: 'And you have undeniable, documented proof of all this?'

Smanski said: 'Would I be calling you if I didn't? I just wanted to give you a heads-up, Dennis. We've always played square with each other and you know how much I respect President Evers, if not some of his staff.'

'The feeling's mutual, I assure you.' DeWitt gazed absently out of his office window for a moment. 'I don't suppose you'd hold off tonight's special broadcast until I can speak to the President?'

'Sorry.'

'What if I could arrange an emergency meeting in the Oval Office — say within the hour? Would you be willing to discuss this with him in person?'

'Hold on a moment, Dennis, I'll ask.' Smanski turned to Ben and Hunter. 'He wants to know if we'd be willing to meet with President Evers right away.'

'Who's going to guarantee our safety?' said Ben.

'Would a police escort work for you?'

Ben and Hunter swapped looks.

'Guys, I honestly doubt if the President will have us all shot in the Oval Office.'

Ben shrugged. 'Your call, Hunter.'

She chewed on it for another moment. Then she nodded and said: 'Okay — we're in.'

20

An hour later Erin Scudder entered the Oval Office. President Evers was standing by the window, staring out across the lawn. She said: 'I'm sorry to keep you waiting, sir, but the photo op took longer than ex — '

Her voice trailed off as she realized that the President had visitors, four of them, all seated on a couch with coffee set out before them. She recognized Smanski, Janelle Freeman and —

A chill raised gooseflesh on her arms as she also recognized Hunter and Ben.

'Sit down, Erin,' said the President.

Recovering, she said: 'Mr. President, I need to talk to you first — '

Evers turned away from the window and pinned her with a look. 'Sit. *Down*.'

She sat, trying not to show the panic she felt.

'I think you know everyone here,' said Evers. He picked Hunter's report up from his desk and waved it at Scudder. 'Detective Hicks and Ms. McCormack have accused you of a heinous crime, Erin. You, General Trilling and other members of the Utopians.'

Mention of the name seemed to strike her like a blow. 'Mr. President, I — '

'Don't bother to deny it. Everything is documented in here, and tonight Ms. Freeman will go public with the findings on a special news broadcast.'

Scudder's lips worked, but nothing came out.

'Your political career is over and so, possibly, is mine. I may not have known what was going on but as chief cook and bottle washer I'm responsible for everything that happens on my watch.'

'M-Mr. President — ' she began.

Evers angrily cut her off. 'Goddammit, woman, how could you have stood by while this experimental genocide took place?'

Lowering her head, she said through sudden tears: 'I didn't realize . . . The way General Trilling described the big picture, it sounded great. Killing off militants

. . . keeping the world safe . . . but then it got out of control and I didn't know how to stop it.'

'*I* could have stopped it,' said President Evers, grinding out every word. 'If you'd had the guts to come to me. But no. You closed your eyes to everything — murder . . . a bombing . . . Ms. McCormack and Detective Hicks being hunted like rabid dogs . . . ' Words seemed to fail him, but only for a moment. 'May God forgive you, Erin, because I certainly can't. And I'm sure a jury won't, either.'

He pressed the intercom switch. 'Send them in, Mrs. Rutledge.'

An inner door opened and two Secret Service agents entered. Erin looked up at them, then across the room at President Evers. There was only contempt in his expression as he said: 'Get her out of my sight.'

'As for myself,' the President continued once she'd left, 'I plan to resign.'

Silence filled the room. It was clear that no one wanted to be there. Then Hunter said: 'Mr. President, may I say something? Your resignation would only further cripple this country.'

'Hunter's right, Mr. President,' Ben said. 'When this gets out most of the world is going to view us with revulsion. We'll need your strength to pull us through.'

President Evers looked less than impressed by the sentiment. 'Thanks for the vote of confidence. But once this hits the airwaves and my opponents in Congress team up to decide my fate, I may not have a choice. In fact, I shall probably be impeached.'

* * *

General Trilling took her eye away from the microscope, straightened up and turned to the two scientists standing beside her.

'Could this be a mistake?' she asked quietly.

Dr. Lu shook her head. 'No, General. Dr. Myorski and I both agree: this is definitely a cloned human embryo that has no head.'

'Can you keep it alive?'

'We believe so,' Dr. Myorski said. 'Of course, we're still very much in the experimental stage, but — ' she broke off as the General's cell phone buzzed.

General Trilling took out her phone and said: 'Speak.' She listened for a moment, her face darkening, and then asked: 'What is your ETA, Captain? . . . Very well. Outside, at the entrance.' She ended the call and turned to Myorski and Lu. 'You and your staff are to remain here, in the lab, until I tell you differently.'

'What is it, General?' Dr. Lu asked. 'What's wrong?'

'Just obey my orders,' General Trilling snapped. 'And under no circumstances are you to tell anyone about this latest experiment. Is that clear?' Before the two scientists could more than nod, Trilling motioned for her aide to follow her and hurried from the lab.

Swapping uneasy looks, Dr. Myorski and Dr. Lu went to the window.

Outside, nothing had changed. The mob of angry, signbearing protesters were still gathered beyond the chainlink fence and the gate; and the club-wielding security guards and guard-dog handlers were still lined up ready to repel them. Television camera crews were taping everything. Parked behind them were several vans with dishantennas on their roofs and the logos of the local TV stations emblazoned on their doors.

Then, shortly, three black SUVs peeled off the highway and roared toward the main gate. As the vehicles approached, the protesters turned to meet them. Yelling and waving their signs threateningly, they at first refused to allow the SUVs to pass. But when the tinted windows were lowered and firearms were aimed at them, the mob grudgingly separated, allowing the vehicles to reach the gate.

General Trilling and Lieutenant Avery stood outside the entrance to Biotech Industries and watched as the SUVs pulled up in front of them.

Captain Colby and her squad spilled out of the vehicles and lined up before the General. All wore steel helmets, body armor and were armed with automatic weapons.

'How close is the column, Captain?'
'Less than five minutes away, General.'
'Estimated size of force?'
'I counted six trucks, ma'am. Perhaps sixty or seventy men.'
'Who's in command, do you know?'
'According to our sources, Colonel Alec Windham.'
'A weekend warrior,' General Trilling said disparagingly. 'How the mighty have fallen.'
'Ma'am, Colonel Windham served two tours in Iraq and Afghanistan and was awarded the Silver Star and a Purple Heart for gallantry in action. May I advise we don't take him too lightly?'
General Trilling gave Colby a withering look and then ordered her to deploy her squad so that no one entered or left the building.
Colby looked uneasy. 'Am I to understand that if necessary, the General wants us to open fire on the National Guard?'
'Do you or any of your squad have a problem with that?' Before the captain could reply, General Trilling added: 'Must I remind you, Captain, that when you

joined the Utopians you swore allegiance to our group and agreed to obey any order you were given.'

'I've not forgotten that, ma'am. Nor was I suggesting that I or my squad would not obey your orders. I just wanted to be absolutely clear as to what extent the General expected us to go.'

'I 'expect' you and your squad to protect, with your lives if necessary, the world-changing experiments that have been performed in Biotech's lab. Is that clear enough for you?'

'Perfectly, ma'am.'

Saluting, Capt. Colby rejoined her squad and began deploying them both inside and outside the building.

'General, look.' Lieutenant Avery pointed toward the gate, where a Jeep-led column of six covered trucks full of soldiers had just pulled up.

General Trilling eyed her adversaries in grim silence.

'General, they have no right to treat you like this. Not after all your years of dedicated service.'

General Trilling looked at her aide

and sighed bitterly. 'Sometimes, Jill, even dedication isn't enough. Now, take your position.'

'Yes, ma'am.' Avery saluted and moved off.

General Trilling remained where she was. Facing the driveway on which the column was now advancing, she opened the holster at her hip and took out her stainless steel, ivory-handled 9mm semi automatic. Cocking it, she held it at her side and stared fixedly at the approaching column.

Shortly, the Jeep and trucks pulled up in front of her. Colonel Windham, a tall, hard-bellied man with steely eyes, got down from the Jeep and barked an order. Immediately the soldiers piled out of the trucks and, weapons ready, formed a line facing the entrance.

General Trilling did not move as Colonel Windham confronted her and saluted. 'General, I must ask you and your militia to surrender your weapons.'

'And if we don't?'

'Then, ma'am, I am ordered to take them by force.'

General Trilling did not respond.

The silence was filled with high-voltage tension as the National Guardsmen and Captain Colby and her squad waited for General Trilling's answer.

'General,' Colonel Windham said finally, 'I'm asking you for the last time: put down your weapons.'

'It's too late for that,' General Trilling said. Even as she spoke she quickly raised her gun hand, pressed the muzzle under her chin — and pulled the trigger.

21

Beneath the studio lights, Janelle composed herself as her director counted her in.

'Stand by . . . five . . . four . . . three . . . two, and . . . *go!*'

Janelle smiled into the cameras.

'Good evening. I'm Janelle Freeman. Tonight, instead of our regular news program we are bringing you a special two-hour broadcast entitled: 'Tomorrow, Utopia.'

Videotape showed a remote refugee camp in Chad, where UN soldiers were handing out food and water from trucks to starving refugees, all of them female.

'It is a shocking story, ladies and gentlemen . . . and certainly not one of which the United States can be proud . . . But we are, if nothing else, a nation who believes in the truth.'

The picture changed to piles of male refugee corpses being dumped into a communal grave, while wives and children looked on, weeping inconsolably.

'We demand it, in fact. Not only from ourselves but from others . . . and we will go to extraordinary lengths to uncover the truth, no matter how much embarrassment or disgrace we have to endure . . . '

The image changed to a shot of the Potomac River at dawn, and an empty scull floating half-submerged in the water beside a wooden dock.

'Our story begins along the banks of the Potomac, one of the most beautiful and historic rivers in America. It was here that Senator Joseph Walsh was drowned by an unknown assailant . . . '

The screen now showed Captain Colby's squad of women surrendering their weapons to National Guardsmen . . . although there was no sign of Captain Colby herself. It was followed by shots of Drs. Lu and Myorski being escorted to an awaiting police car, while cheering protestors looked on.

'Senator Walsh was a staunch opponent of human embryonic stem cell research, as were his colleagues, Senator Cobb and

Congressmen Jacobs and Stankowski . . . who were killed in a bombing that at first was attributed to Neo-Nazi skinheads but in fact was committed by a group of women known as The Utopians . . .'

A series of shots of General Trilling, on duty in Iraq and being interviewed outside the Pentagon, showed on the television screen.

'Their leader was General Katherine Trilling. Recently promoted, and only one of two women to ever become a four-star general, she chose death rather than face disgrace and life imprisonment . . .'

The image changed again: a tearful Erin Scudder, looking out through a car window as she was taken away from the White House by the Secret Service.

'Why were these politicians, and other innocent victims whom we'll describe later in the program, murdered?'

On-screen appeared a photograph of Hunter, taken several years earlier by NSA for identification purposes.

'We might never have known the answer but for the courage and tenacity of this woman, Hunter McCormack, a cryptologist at the Pentagon . . . '

Ben's face appeared.

' . . . and this man, Detective Ben Hicks of the Metropolitan Police Force. Despite being targeted by General Trilling's assassins, they risked their lives to expose a multi-billion-dollar military plot to develop a synthetic cancer-causing virus that, when perfected, would have resulted in the mass-slaughter of millions of militants, terrorists and other enemies of the state . . . '

* * *

Hunter and Ben sat at the counter eating sushi in the Golden Bowl, a Japanese restaurant on Florida Avenue. As they ate they watched Janelle's special on the television mounted on the wall facing them. The sound was off and suddenly the program was interrupted by a special news broadcast showing Captain Colby's squad, unarmed and with their hands up, being escorted out of the Biotech building by National Guardsmen. There was still no sign of Captain Colby.

'I can't believe General Trilling shot herself,' Hunter said. 'She just didn't seem the type to take the short way home.'

Ben shrugged. 'Death before dishonor,' he replied.

'It's sad, really. She's done so much for women in the military — *and* for her country. To have her legacy end like this . . . well, it's just very sad.'

Ben nodded and then indicated the clock on the wall. 'If I'm going to make that meeting, we have to get going.' He dug some money from his wallet and left it atop the check.

Outside, as they were getting into his car, it suddenly hit Hunter. 'That's odd,' she said.

Ben paused in the middle of fastening his seat belt, 'What is?' and then buckled up.

'The blonde — the one who killed Andy — she wasn't with them.'

'Probably holed up somewhere.'

Hunter wasn't convinced. As they drove off, she said: 'Someone like her, a hardcore radical, an assassin, it doesn't make sense. She'd want to be right there, beside her leader.'

'Maybe she was there and we just didn't see her — or maybe she was off-camera when the media was taping.'

'Maybe,' Hunter said, still not completely persuaded.

★ ★ ★

About twenty minutes later Ben stood outside the meeting hall where he'd previously attended his AA meetings. Traffic passed behind him and a cool evening breeze swirled litter around his shoes. Taking a deep breath, he forced himself to open the door and enter.

The alcoholics seated in rows before the podium all turned and looked at him. Ben managed a weak smile and nodding to a few faces he recognized — including young Billy Padgett — then took an empty seat in the back row. Everyone faced front again, and continued to listen to the speaker.

Seated at the end of the back row, next to the aisle leading to the front door, was a trim, hard-faced woman with short dark hair, gold-rimmed glasses and cold brown eyes. Despite makeup and a smart dark-blue dress, she seemed more manly than feminine, and fidgeted as if self-conscious in her present attire. She'd kept her head down as Ben squeezed past her to get to his seat, and Ben, his mind on what he would have to announce shortly, barely noticed her.

When the speaker was finished, he looked at Ben and smiled.

Everyone was silent.

Ben sat there, wondering if he was doing the right thing. But what the hell — he went ahead and did it anyway.

Rising, he said: 'I'm Detective Ben Hicks . . . and I'm an alcoholic.'

Everyone applauded.

* * *

When Ben left the meeting hall, Hunter was outside, waiting for him with a big hug. 'How did it go?'

'Better than I expected.'

'I'm proud of you,' she said. 'I always hoped that one day my dad would stand up and admit he was an alcoholic, but he never did — '

'Congratulations, Detective Hicks!'

Hunter and Ben turned and looked at the dark-haired woman who'd just emerged from the hall.

'Thanks,' Ben began. 'I — '

Hunter cut him off. 'Y-You,' she said, recognizing the woman.

'That's right — me,' said Irene Colby, aiming her gun at them.

'Aw, fuck,' muttered Ben.

'And since you know who I am, Hunter, you also know I won't hesitate to use this if you don't do exactly as I say.'

She removed her glasses and black wig, revealing short tawny blonde hair, and motioned for them to walk ahead of her.

Grudgingly, they obeyed. As they entered the parking lot, their shadows gliding alongside them, the captain extended her free hand to Ben, saying: 'I'll take your weapon, Detective.'

Without argument Ben handed his gun to her. She tucked it in her pocket and continued to keep them both covered as they walked toward Ben's car.

'How come you weren't at Biotech with your beloved general?' Hunter asked over her shoulder.

'I was,' Colby said, 'right up to the moment she blew her head off. Then I realized she wasn't the person I thought she was and it was every woman for herself.'

They'd reached Ben's car. They stopped and Ben indicated his inside breast pocket. 'I could use a drink,' he said.

Hunter looked shocked. 'Ben — '

'What?' he said, adding: 'What fucking difference is it gonna make now, baby?'

He looked at Colby.

'Typical man,' she sneered, 'weak to the last.' Then she nodded for him to go ahead. 'Nice 'n' easy,' she warned as he reached into his jacket. 'Don't try to be a hero.'

Hunter looked on, anguished, as Ben pulled out a pint of J.D., unscrewed the top and, pausing momentarily, finally took a swig. He gave a long, shuddery sigh, 'Man, that's more like it,' then went to return the bottle to his pocket. As he did, the bottle hit his lapel and slipped from his fingers. He grabbed for it but the bottle smashed on the asphalt. 'Shit.'

Colby grinned. 'Seems like the gods are against you, soldier.'

'Fuck 'em,' Ben said. 'I got more in the car.' He turned and opened the car door, intending to get in.

'Hold it,' Colby said. Then to Hunter: 'You get in first. And don't fuck with me,' she added when Hunter didn't move, 'or you'll get it right here.'

Reluctantly, Hunter walked around and got in on the passenger side.

'Okay, now you, soldier,' Colby said to Ben.

As he got in behind the wheel, she climbed in the back seat and pressed the gun against Hunter's head. 'Drive,' she told Ben. 'And remember, you pull any cute stunts and I'll paint her brains all over the windshield.'

'No stunts,' he assured her, and his voice cracked. 'But I do need another drink.' Without waiting for her permission, he reached across Hunter and opened the glove compartment.

Colby's finger tightened around the trigger. She watched intently as Ben pulled out a half-empty fifth of J.D. and held it up, saying: 'Either of you ladies care to join me?' His bravado slipped, then. 'Might ease the pain a little, Hunter,' he added. 'You know, when it comes to it.'

Hunter turned away, even more disgusted.

Colby chuckled. 'Seems like you've offended your girlfriend, soldier.'

For a fleeting moment Ben looked ashamed, but then unscrewed the cap. 'Win some, lose some,' he said belligerently. He took a drink, replaced the cap and put the bottle back into the glove compartment. 'Okay,' he said, half-turning toward Colby, 'where we going?'

Before she could answer, he shot her between the eyes with the snub-nosed .38 Smith & Wesson now in his hand.

The bullet slammed her back, blood welling from a neat round hole in her forehead. She was dead before she slumped against the seat.

'You all right?' Ben asked Hunter.

Her ears still ringing from the closely-confined explosion, Hunter nodded dumbly.

Ben returned the gun to the clamp in the glove compartment. He then got out his cell, speed-dialed the station and reported what had happened. Hunter got out of the car with him, not wanting to spend any more time than she had to with the corpse.

When he was finished, he turned back to Hunter and she crushed herself against him, trembling. After a while he reached back into the car and took out the bottle. 'Here,' he said, 'take a swig. It's great for what ails you.'

'That's not funny,' she said.

'I'm not joking,' he replied seriously.

After a moment of hesitation, Hunter wiped the top of the bottle with her sleeve and drank. 'Tell me something, Ben, and I want it straight. Does this mean you're back on the — ?'

' — sauce?' he said. 'No.'

'But just for a moment there I thought — '

'Once an alcoholic always an alcoholic?'

'Don't tell me it's not true.'

'I'm not. But I'm *not* an alcoholic, Hunter. I've *never* been an alcoholic. What I am — what I *used to be* — is a lush.'

'There's a difference?'

'A big one. An alcoholic is someone who drinks because they can't stop. A lush is someone who drinks because they *want* to drink.'

'I get it,' she said skeptically. 'You can stop any time you like, is that it?'

'Stick around and see for yourself,' he invited, and plucking the bottle from her hand, he up-ended it and watched the contents slosh into the gutter. 'Does that answer your question?' he asked when the bottle was empty.

'One of them,' she said, her voice suddenly husky.

'Well, when you think of some others,' he said, pulling her close again, 'just ask away.'

He kissed her then . . . and was still kissing her when the cops showed up five minutes later.

THE END

Other titles in the
Linford Mystery Library:

THE RETURN OF MR. BUDD

Gerald Verner

Near Avernley in Berkshire, Superintendent Budd of Scotland Yard is relaxing on holiday at the cottage of his friend, Jacob Mutch. However, Mr. Budd becomes involved in an investigation. He learns from Jacob's neighbour that his cottage has been burgled — twice. Yet nothing was taken. Then the man is found in his cottage brutally murdered. And the following day, the body of a known criminal is found dead nearby, shot through the head!

FOREIGN ASSIGNMENT

Sydney J. Bounds

In the unstable Congo region of Africa, the state of Katanga is an oasis of calm. President Tshombe and his government are united; the country's mines and industries supply the West with copper and uranium. But others, who stand to benefit if the government go under, have plans to assassinate the President. Meanwhile, Detective Simon Brand must prevent the assassination and root out the men behind the plot — and he has just seventy-two hours in which to do it . . .

MOTIVE FOR MURDER

John Russell Fearn

Inspector Mallison was reluctant to arrest the murdered man's son, although the incriminating evidence was overwhelming: he'd been alone with his father immediately prior to the murder and there'd been a bitter quarrel; Goldstein was killed trying to alter his will — unfavourably for his son; the weapon, a desk paperweight bore the son's fingerprints, and his father had withdrawn financial support for a new West End play in which his son was to star. Yet still Mallinson wasn't convinced . . .

RETRIBUTION

Norman Lazenby

Mary Calvin sits in her flat for hours, full of fury and sick with despair for the dreadful waste of her friend's young life, Evelyn Torrance. A dreadful resolution begins to dominate her mind: retribution! Fred Tanner must pay for his crime! She takes sleeping tablets from the medicine chest and selecting a sharp ornamental dagger from the mantelshelf, she slips them into her handbag. She puts on her coat, hurries out and heads for Tanner's flat . . .